Book II

By Lindsay Uvery

 FriesenPress

Suite 300 - 990 Fort St
Victoria, BC, V8V 3K2
Canada

www.friesenpress.com

Copyright © 2017 by Lindsay Uvery
First Edition — 2017

All rights reserved.

No part of this publication may be reproduced in any form, or by any means, electronic or mechanical, including photocopying, recording, or any information browsing, storage, or retrieval system, without permission in writing from FriesenPress.

ISBN
978-1-5255-0683-3 (Hardcover)
978-1-5255-0684-0 (Paperback)
978-1-5255-0685-7 (eBook)

1. FICTION, FANTASY

Distributed to the trade by The Ingram Book Company

MOON'S TALE: BIRTH OF THE HYBRID

My name is Liz, and this year I found out I was part-werewolf, part-vampire and part-witch. If that isn't weird enough, I also just gave birth to a hybrid baby in my own home! So now here I am living with vampires and running away from other vampires and humans. I recently found out that my dad is a vampire and was a king, and my brother is also a vampire— possibly a hybrid like me. My mother was queen, and she is a witch and a werewolf. All these years I thought I had no family, but I ended up running into them. My whole life has been turned upside down in such a short time. And those other girls bitch about how their parents got a divorce and how they are getting fat and their boyfriend just broke up with them. Reality check— try being a werewolf and a vampire! It isn't as rosy as one would think.

Now that you know the story, shall I began?

Chapter 1

THE DEAL

I was standing back waiting for the two male vampires to start talking to me, but instead they stood there staring at me, holding my baby daughter Celina. I just looked at my watch and sighed before looking around at my surroundings. It wasn't the nicest out—the wind was whistling in my ears and the rain was coming down hard. I could barely see two feet in front of me. I was starting to get pissed off. This wasn't my idea of trying to make a deal, but I needed my child back. I wanted to be sitting with my family enjoying a hot cup of cocoa.

"Hey, what's going on?" I asked. I stepped closer to see if I could recognize the men.

"We were waiting to see if it was actually you," one man spoke as he lit a cigarette.

"Did you have to wait that long? It isn't beach weather, you know," I snarled as I hugged myself, shivering.

"Anyways, dear, are you ready to make a deal? You did come alone, didn't you?" the man who was holding my baby asked me as he stepped closer.

"Yes, I did come alone. I am not stupid," I snapped. I smelled the air around me. It was cold and it made it hard to breathe.

"We want the diamond you have in exchange for your baby," the man said.

"What diamond?" I asked, confused.

"Don't play dumb— you know what I am talking about," the man hissed as he dug around in his pockets for something.

"Seriously, I have never seen this diamond you have mentioned," I said. I took a step towards the men.

"Alright, have it your way," the man replied. Suddenly, two other men jumped out of the car that was parked beside us and grabbed me. I just stood there and started laughing.

"What's so funny?" the man asked as he backhanded me.

"You will soon find out," I snapped. I spit in his face.

He wiped the spit off and growled at me. Soon all the vampires started covering their ears and dropping to the ground. I could hear Celina cry. I ran over and grabbed her, and then jumped in my car and sped off. I couldn't believe the adrenaline that was running through my body.

I eventually made it home in one piece. The rain was still coming down and I could barely see to park my car. I picked up my baby from her car seat in the backseat and ran inside the house, locking the door behind me.

"Liz, you made it," my mom said as she ran towards me and hugged me. She took Celina out of my arms. The whole family was there: Mom and Dad, my brothers, Celina's dad Kelvin and the rest of the guys.

"Yeah, thanks to you, Mom," I replied, smiling.

"What did they want?" my dad asked as he stood up to come see Celina.

"They wanted a diamond," I replied with a confused gesture.

"They are still after that diamond," Jeff replied as he took a sip of a glass filled with blood.

"What is so important about this diamond?" I asked. I took my Celina to see if they hurt her.

"The diamond is supposed to break them from the curse of being unable to walk in daylight," Jeff explained.

"I thought some of them could," I said, confused again.

"If they have a witch cast a spell on them once they are turned, they can," Jeff explained.

"I don't know where this diamond is anyways," I replied. I sat down on the couch next to Kelvin.

"We have it here, but your mother put a spell on it so it can't fall into the wrong hands," Mark answered.

"Oh, that is reassuring," I said as I kissed my Celina.

"Anyways, enough about the diamond. Let's look at Celina," my dad said, sitting down beside me.

I unraveled her from the blanket and she started to cry. I pulled her close to me, tapping her lightly on her back and bouncing her a bit.

"I wonder if she is hungry," Kelvin said as he went into the kitchen.

"Maybe, but I have no baby stuff," I replied. I looked at the time to see if it was too late to grab some supplies for her.

"No worries, we got it for you," my brother Hunter replied as he came into the room and handed me some bags.

"Thanks so much," I said. I handed Celina over to Hunter so I could rummage through the bags.

"We should make her a bottle now," I said. Hunter handed Celina over to Kelvin and I headed into the kitchen. I grabbed a bottle, rinsed it out, put some blood in it and turned on the microwave to warm it up a bit. I could hear the baby crying and Kelvin trying to calm her down, but she just cried harder.

"Liz, hurry up, please!" Kelvin yelled.

"I'm coming! I'm just warming up her food!" I yelled back. I took the bottle out of the microwave and went in to the living room. I took Celina from Kelvin and just laughed at him.

"What's so funny?" Kelvin asked, looking annoyed.

"You don't know how to handle a baby when it's upset," I replied as I put the bottle in her mouth. She must have been hungry, because she almost drank the whole bottle. After she was done eating I walked around patting her on the back until she burped.

"I guess we can lay her down to sleep now. The crib is upstairs, but we still need to set it up. Come on, dear," my mom said as she went upstairs. I handed Kelvin to Celina and followed my mom upstairs to give her a hand.

"Mother, how come you left me at such a young age?" I asked as we set up the crib.

"I didn't want you to live your life running away all the time. I wanted what was best for you," my mom replied.

"In the past year that is all I have been doing. I finally escape then another group of vampires come into place and kidnap me and torture me," I replied.

We got the crib set up. "There," my mom said. "Finally done. And honey, I know, but it was bound to happen…you can't deny what you are. You have to think of it as a gift. Use it to your advantage, but never let it control your life." She kissed my cheek and went downstairs.

I just stood there and thought about what my mom said. I knew she was right, but it was hard to think of it as a gift. Now I had a baby to raise, and those other vampires would stop at nothing until they got that diamond. I went downstairs to bring Celina up to bed.

"Here, I will take Celina now. She is probably tired," I said as I took her away from Kelvin and went back upstairs. I lay her down in the crib and just watched her. She looked up at me with those big blue eyes and smiled. I couldn't believe she was mine.

+ + +

"Liz sure has gotten stronger in the past few months," Hunter said.

"Yeah, she has, and she will only get stronger," Blair replied.

"She is capable of so much," Hunter said.

"That she is, and I am afraid for her," Blair replied.

"We all are," Jeff said, butting into the conversation.

"I am going to go upstairs and talk to Liz and see my baby," Kelvin said as he stood up and headed upstairs.

+ + +

I was still standing there watching Celina as she slept when I heard someone behind me.

"Who is there?" I asked as I turned around.

"Kelvin," Kelvin replied as he came closer to look at Celina.

"Isn't she beautiful?" I asked, smiling.

"Yes, like you," Kelvin replied as he looked at me.

I smiled and kissed Kelvin. "Thanks."

We left Celina to sleep and went back downstairs. I had just sat back down when my phone rang. I answered it. "Hello," I said.

"Hello. I know this is Liz, and if you think we have forgotten about our deal, think again, sweetheart, because we know where you are. If I were you I would stop playing games and give us what we want or things will get nasty," the voice hissed and hung up.

"Who was that?" Hunter asked as I slammed my phone down on the coffee table.

"Those stupid vampires wanting their stupid diamond," I replied, crossing my arms.

"I hate to be the bearer of bad news, but I don't think they will give up," Hunter said.

"I know…they are stubborn," I replied.

"Tyler, Steven, you don't have to stay here," I said, looked at my human friends, who were also there at the house.

"I know, but we don't have anywhere to go right now," Steven answered.

"Alright, well, as long as you guys are okay staying with vampires, you are more than welcome," I replied, smiling.

"I remember when I first met you," Tyler reminisced. "Your beautiful smile, gorgeous eyes, cute laugh, sexy body, and of course the part of you that's a werewolf. I miss the first time we made love. I miss cuddling up to your warm body."

He was talking about the good times we had when we first met. Tyler started crying; he felt bad for letting me go just because I was half-vampire.

"I know, Tyler, but I stuck with your decision. I didn't want to force you to be with me if you didn't want to," I replied.

"I know. It was a foolish mistake. I was being selfish. I hated vampires so much because they toyed around with my parents and my siblings… my siblings and I got away, but my parents didn't stand a chance," Tyler explained as he looked at me.

"You didn't tell me that. I am sorry that happened." I got up and went back into the kitchen.

Tyler got up and followed me. "I didn't tell you because I hated talking about it. I needed to be stronger and I needed to let it go. It was in the past," Tyler explained as he stood beside me.

"I understand. Sometimes we need to talk about it. If we keep it a secret it will just build up until one day we snap," I said as I poured some water into the sink.

"I know. I am bad with my emotions," Tyler said as Hunter walked in.

"I know. I am not the best at them either," I replied as I started washing the dishes.

"Liz, it is late. You should go get some sleep. It has been a busy day for you," Hunter suggested as he took over for me.

"Yeah, you are probably right… besides, I have to wake up early with Celina," I said. I dried my hands off and headed upstairs. I had a shower and brushed my hair and teeth. I slipped on a nightgown and crawled into bed. A few minutes later Kelvin joined me.

"Hey, honey?" I said as I rolled over.

"Hey, babe," Kelvin replied as he rolled over to face me.

"I am so glad I met you," I said as I touched Kelvin's face. He smiled and kissed my hand.

"I am glad I met you too. You are my world, baby," Kelvin replied and he held on to me.

"I hope you guys never leave me," I said as I let out a yawn.

"Never. Even if you end up in the hospital, one of us will always be there," Kelvin replied as he gently kissed my lips and caressed my body.

I couldn't stand it any longer. I started forcefully kissing him as I rolled on top of him. He felt me up as he took my nightgown off. I took his boxers off and he inserted himself into me. It had been so long since I had sex. I was moaning and kissing him. He flipped me over and he was on top. After we made love we just lay there in complete silence for awhile.

"You're so sexy," Kelvin said as he stared into my blue eyes.

"You are too," I said. I chuckled a bit.

We soon fell asleep in each other's arms. I woke up a few hours later and patted the spot next to me—Kelvin was gone. I sat up and got out of bed. I could hear fighting downstairs. I wasn't in a huge rush to see what was going on, but I got dressed and went downstairs enough to see who was there. I didn't want anyone else to know I was there.

It was Natasha… oh no, this could not be good.

"I thought you were only going to be here for a few hours!" Natasha screeched as she shoved Kelvin.

"What, I can't spend time with my friends?" Kelvin asked angrily.

"I think there is more going on. I think Liz is back—I can smell her dog scent all over you," Natasha snapped as she looked around to see if she could see me.

"How did you know Liz was even gone?" Kelvin asked, obviously mad.

"Because I told those vampires where she was. I wanted her gone!" Natasha shouted.

"You bitch," Kelvin said, in shock.

"You have no idea," Natasha replied as she made her hands into fists.

I watched from the stairs as Hunter came up to them. "Natasha, calm down, we don't need any trouble. How about we talk about this rationally?" he suggested, coming in between them.

"Hunter, tell me, is Liz back?' Natasha asked.

"That doesn't matter. Let's just calm down," Hunter replied, looking quite annoyed at this point.

"No, I will not calm down until I find out what is going on with Liz!" Natasha screamed as she started throwing things around. All of a sudden she dropped to the floor holding her head. My mom was right behind her.

"That is enough, dear. Please come back when you have calmed down," she said as she helped Natasha out the door.

That's when I came downstairs. I really didn't want to interfere this time.

"I am sorry for causing so much grief," I muttered as I walked past my mom and the boys.

"No, don't think that way," all three said at the same time.

I just shook my head and laughed. I went into the kitchen, opened up the fridge and scoped it out. "What do I want to eat? Maybe I should warm up some blood for Celina," I mumbled to myself as I reached for a bottle. I was about to poor blood into it when I was interrupted.

"What are you doing, Liz?' Kelvin asked as he stepped behind me and wrapped his arms around my waist.

"I am getting Celina's bottle ready," I replied, giggling.

"I fed her already. I had her up and fed. Now she is playing with grandpa," Kelvin explained as he smiled.

"Thanks, honey, you are a wonderful dad. I love you," I said, smiling back.

"Thanks, babe, I love you too," Kelvin replied.

I left the kitchen and headed back upstairs to check on Celina.

+ + +

"You really love her," Hunter said to Kelvin.

"Yes, I do. I wanted to be with her. You sound shocked," Kelvin replied with a puzzled look.

"Well, it's just that Liz deserves to be loved and she hasn't had that from a guy. I mean, yeah, she has family but she needs a man to love her too, in that intimate way. She had Tyler, but he didn't accept her for who she was," Hunter explained. He smiled and came towards Kelvin and patted him on the back.

"I heard that entire speech, Hunter," said Tyler, walking in the room. "No, you are right, I didn't accept her. I mean, how can I? She is a bloodsucker. At the same time, I look at Liz and it rips me apart knowing that I threw her away." Tyler was fighting back the tears.

"What is done is done—you can't change the past, but you can change the future," Hunter replied as he left the kitchen and headed upstairs.

"What did he mean by that?" Tyler asked Kelvin as they stood in the kitchen.

"I think what Hunter means is next time you find a girl that you want in your life, you should learn from your mistakes and accept her for who she is, and what she is," Kelvin explained as he went into the living room.

Tyler just stood there for a few seconds and wandered into the living room. "Yeah, you're right. I just panicked. When Liz told me what she was I was being selfish," he admitted.

"At least you can admit and you realize it…that is important," Kelvin answered as he flipped through the TV channels.

+ + +

"Hey Liz, how are you making out?" Hunter asked as he put his arm around me. We both looked at Celina.

"I am alright, I guess. I mean, I don't know what to do about Natasha...what does she want?" I asked as I looked at Hunter.

"She's jealous. She wants Kelvin, and he doesn't want her. She thinks the only way to have him is to get rid of you," Hunter explained.

"Yeah, your right. Do you think she's a threat?" I asked as I touched Celina's face.

"At this point, I am not sure. She already handed you over; we will just have to watch our backs," Hunter replied.

"I know. I just don't want to cause any trouble," I muttered. I stepped out of the room. Hunter followed me and we both headed back downstairs and sat on the couch where Tyler and Kelvin were hanging out.

"Where is everyone else?" I asked as I looked around.

"I don't know. They were gone when I got up," Hunter answered.

Soon the door opened and Damien, Trent, Mark, Jeff, Steven and Blair came walking in with grocery bags.

"Where did you guys go?" I asked. I got up and took some of the bags and put them on the kitchen table.

"We did some shopping," Damien answered.

I unpacked the bags and put away the groceries and baby food. "Where's my mother?" I asked, confused

"I'm not sure. Did you check downstairs?" Blair answered.

"No, I will go check," I replied. I opened the basement door and walked down the old stairs. I saw my mother in the spare room cross-legged and it looked like she was praying.

"Hello, dear," Jane said as she stopped what she was doing and looked up at me.

"Hello, Mom. What are you doing?" I asked as I say beside her.

"I am putting extra protection on you and the family. I can feel those vampires coming, and they are getting ready for war," Jane warned me and continued what she was doing.

I didn't even argue or say anything. I stood up and left her be. When I headed back upstairs I heard a knock at the door— talk about butterflies.

Chapter 2

SURPRISE

I stood there hoping the person or monster on the other side of the door would take the hint and leave us alone, but the knocking continued, getting louder and louder.

"Holy shit. Coming!" Hunter shouted as he went to open the door.

"No, Hunter!" I yelled as I ran in front of him.

"Liz, there is someone at the door," Hunter said as he tried pushing me out of the way.

"Wait until mother is done her spell. I have a bad feeling about this," I whispered.

Hunter looked quite annoyed. Soon there was complete silence and I was sure the people knocking gave up. I sighed in relief and moved out the way. As soon as I got relaxed there was a huge crash through the living room window, and glass flew everywhere.

"What the fuck," Blair shouted as all of the guys stood up and backed away from the glass.

"Hello, you fucks, came to take what is mine— the girl and the diamond," the man who broke in commanded.

"No! It can't be Caleb," I said, shocked.

"Baby, you actually thought I would forget about my sweet, sweet hybrid princess," Caleb growled as he grabbed me and pulled me close to him.

I was so pissed off I did something even I never thought I was capable of doing. I stared right into Caleb's eyes and raised my arm then moved it back really fast. Caleb went flying across the living room right into the kitchen. He got up, laughing as he stood there for a few seconds, and then he came walking towards me.

"Well, dear, it looks like you met your mother Jane and she taught you some mother-and-daughter bonding," Caleb said, still laughing as he grabbed me by my hair and dragged me to the broken window.

"Leave her alone," Kelvin shouted as he lunged at Caleb.

Caleb shifted into a wolf as Kelvin lunged at Caleb. He moved out of the way then grabbed Kelvin by one arm, lifted him up and bit down on his neck. Kelvin screamed in agony then he was dropped on the ground. "No, you asshole!" I shouted as I shifted into my lycan form. I leaped at Caleb and we fought, bashing into the walls and breaking everything in sight. There was blood everywhere. I was just about to lunge at Caleb when we both hit the floor in pain and shifted back into humans. "What the…" I muttered as I slowly stood up. I was so stiff.

My mom was standing there, and she looked very pissed off. "Stop acting like a bunch of rabid dogs," Jane snarled as she lifted me off the floor and gave me a blanket.

Caleb slowly got up and looked around. He laughed a bit. "You sure know how to put up a fight, baby," Caleb said as he walked towards me.

Just then, I remembered what happened to Kelvin. "Kelvin, no!" I snarled as I ran to him. He was lying on the floor, helpless.

"Kelvin, we will figure out a cure. I won't let you die," I said as tears ran off my cheeks and hit his face.

"I want you to know that I will love you always and forever and tell Celina that I love her," Kelvin mumbled. He coughed a few times and then his body became lifeless.

I cuddled up with him and cried. I cried so hard I could barely breathe.

"*You* did this! Why?" I asked, sobbing as I slowly got up and glared at Caleb. I started screaming and everything in the house started shaking. I was unbelievably pissed off. Things started flying off the walls and off the shelves, smashing into the walls. Caleb was speechless. He seemed so intrigued by how strong I was. He stood there with an evil grin and watched, as if to see what I was planning on doing. Then everything just stopped. I was breathing so heavily and my anger was taking up too much energy, so soon I just collapsed.

Caleb began clapping as he walked closer to me. He flipped me over with his foot. "What a shame she has so much power but she doesn't know how to use it. I must say, though, it is very attractive watching her get so angry," Caleb said. He walked away laughing.

"You're a monster," Jeff snapped at Caleb as he ran over to me.

"Thanks. I have been called worse. By the way, I will be coming back for her— this was just the beginning. Next time I will escape with her," Caleb said as he went out the smashed window.

"This is horrible. Someone pick Liz up and lay her on the couch," my dad demanded. He dragged Kelvin downstairs to where my mother did her spells.

But when he got there, my mom wasn't sure she could help. "I don't know if I am powerful enough to bring Kelvin back to life. If I succeed, who know if he will be the same," Jane said as she looked through her spell books.

I woke up with a splitting headache and I forgot what had happened. I slowly sat up and looked around. Hunter was sitting across from me on the chair.

"How are you feeling?" Hunter asked.

"I am weak and tired and my head feels like it weighs a ton, but other than that I am just great," I answered sarcastically.

"The others went to a magic store to see if they can find anything on how to kill Caleb," Hunter said as he touched my face.

"Where is Kelvin?" I asked as I looked around.

"He didn't make it. I am so sorry," Hunter said. He hugged me.

I started bawling into his chest. I could barely breathe and I couldn't stop crying. Hunter just rubbed my back and kept telling me, "everything will be ok" over and over again.

I looked up at him, sniffling, and softly said, "No, it won't be" as I ran upstairs and fell on my bed and continued crying.

I heard footsteps, but I didn't even budge to see who it was.

"Liz, I am sorry about Kelvin," Mark said as he sat on the edge of the bed.

"I want him back. I will miss him so much. This is all my fault," I said as I stood up and punched the wall in anger. I went running downstairs to the basement to see my mother. Kelvin was just lying there motionless.

"Honey, no, I don't want you to see him," my mother said as she stood up to hug me.

"Mom, I want him back," I said as I started crying again.

"Shhh, honey, I know. I am trying to figure out something," my mother replied, trying to comfort me.

"I can't stop crying. Everything reminds me of him," I replied as I looked up at my mother.

"There is one way we can bring him back— if we turn him into a hybrid as well," my mother explained.

"How?" I said, excited.

"Don't get your hopes up, sweetie. I am not sure yet. Give me some time." My mother hugged me and sat down, trying to figure out a hybrid spell.

I sighed and went back upstairs. I was so weak and tired, as all I had been doing was crying. My body ached from the fight I had with Caleb. I wanted to have time to myself. I needed to think. I got my shoes on and left the house.

+ + +

"Hunter, go follow your sister; it is not safe for her out there," Blair demanded to Hunter.

"Alright," Hunter replied as he sighed and left the house.

+ + +

I walked to the nearest riverbank and sat on the bench, just watching the geese and the water flow. The weather was so nice— the sun was shining, the birds were singing and the air around me smelled so fresh.

+ + +

"Where is Liz?" Jane asked as she came running upstairs in excitement.

"She went for a walk. Hunter followed her," Blair replied, looking at her funny.

"I found a way to bring Kelvin back. It isn't going to be easy, though," Jane announced as she went upstairs to check up on Celina. She came back downstairs a few minutes later with Celina in her arms. Jane laid a blanket down with some toys and put Celina on it to play.

+ + +

I had just sat on the bench when I heard my phone go off. It was a new message from my mom. It read "Come back, Liz. I have good news about Kelvin." I smiled a bit and put my phone away. Just as I got up I heard noise coming from the bushes. I smelled around to see if I could tell what is was. It smelled like vampire. *Great*, I thought. I slowly followed the scent and it led right into the bush. I stood on the outside of the bush, too scared to go inside. I waited a few minutes and then someone jumped out at me. I screamed and jumped at least two feet in the air. I realized it was Hunter— he was laughing so hard he could barely breathe.

"You asshole," I snapped as I hit him.

"Come on, Liz, that was too funny," Hunter replied, still laughing.

"Did you follow me?" I asked as we headed back home.

"Yes. It is not safe for you," Hunter replied.

"I know." I sighed as we entered the house. My mom was sitting on the couch, and she jumped up as soon as she saw me walk in.

"Liz, honey, I found a way to bring Kelvin back to life! But it isn't going to be easy." She looked serious.

I waited for a few minutes before she replied. I was giving her that look like, "ok, I'm waiting."

"You have to get blood from the hybrid that killed him, which in this case would be Caleb, then you have to wait for the next full moon and you say this spell. After the spell is repeated a few times, you feed Kelvin Caleb's blood," my mom explained as she pointed the spell out to me.

"Ok, that doesn't sound too hard," I said, shrugging my shoulders.

"That's not all, dear. You need to collect Caleb's blood before tomorrow night at midnight," my mom replied as she closed her spell book.

I stood there in shock. I didn't know how to answer that. "How about I go give myself up to Caleb, then you guys ambush him?" I suggested. I looked at the boys.

"That actually might be our only choice, but we need to plan it out better," Hunter replied as he stood up. Then he fell back down to his chair, putting his head down.

"Are you ok, Hunter?" I asked.

"Yeah, I am fine. Just a little dizzy. It will pass," Hunter replied as he looked up.

"Ok," I said. I went to Celina and picked her up. Jane went into the kitchen to prepare a bottle for Celina as I carried my baby, patting her on the back as I walked around the living room. Soon Jane came out with the bottle and I fed Celina. After burping her I brought her upstairs and lay her down for a nap. I went back downstairs to figure out a plan to get Caleb's blood—it was possible, but getting out of there alive would be another story.

"So, Liz, we were all thinking if you go and hand yourself over to Caleb, your mom will put a tracking spell on you and then we will all ambush him when he has his guard down," Jeff explained.

"How will you know when that is?" I asked, puzzled.

"You will text Hunter this code: 112," Jeff replied as he wrote the code on a piece of paper.

"Ok, that sounds easy enough," I said, but I started to shake.

"We need you to go to him tonight so he doesn't get suspicious. We need him to fall for this," Mark said with a serious tone in his voice.

"Alright, I can't wait," I muttered. I sighed and went upstairs.

+ + +

"I don't like this idea," Hunter said.

"I know. We don't either, but what choice do we have?" Mark replied.

+ + +

I came back downstairs, got my shoes on and made sure I had my phone."Ok, wish me luck. I am basically committing suicide," I said as I left the house.

I wandered down the street. I couldn't remember exactly where he lived, but I could smell him. I went down a back alley and came across this old-looking house. Well, this was where my nose lead me to. I noticed some vampires standing guard.

"Hey, ma'am, you are not allowed in here. This is private property," the one guard said as he blocked the entrance.

"I'm sorry. Let me introduce myself. I am Liz, the female hybrid. I know for a fact if you tell Caleb that I am here waiting for him, he will be out here in a heartbeat," I explained, smiling.

I watched one of the guards talk into a speaker, and shortly after Caleb stepped out.

"Hello, my dear. I knew you would come to your senses and come find me," Caleb said as he smiled and walked towards me. He held onto my wrist and brought me inside. The house was massive on the inside, but it was old and smelled like dust.

"This place is huge, but it smells funny," 'I said as I looked at him.

"You will get use to that smell. Here, let me show you to our room," Caleb replied. I followed him upstairs and he showed me a fairly big room. There was an attached bathroom, a fireplace in one corner, a dresser in the other corner, and the bed had a canopy.

"This bed is beautiful," I said as I laid on it.

"You, my dear, are beautiful," Caleb said as he crawled on top of me.

I just laid there. I had to play along with it, as this was very important. Caleb was facing me and he started kissing me. I kissed him back. I wrapped my arms around him, and he ran his hands up and down my body and over my chest. I moaned a bit as I took his shirt off him, and he did the same for me. Eventually we were naked and we had sex. I felt disgusted with myself, but what choice did I have? I got up and had a shower. After I was done showering, I came back in the room. Caleb was still lying down on the bed.

"Did you even move?" I asked as I got dressed.

"No. I will, though. I am going to go make supper," Caleb replied as he stood up, got dressed and went downstairs. I wasn't far behind him when a vampire and a human walked in—there stood Kevin and Brett, staring at me.

"Liz! Hello, baby," Kevin said as he winked at me.

"Kevin, watch this," Brett said as he grabbed my ass.

"Stop, you sick pervert." I scowled as I went into the kitchen were Caleb was.

"Come on, baby, don't be like that. We were just bugging you," Brett said as they followed me into the kitchen.

"Hey guys, just making some supper. Would you like to join?" Caleb asked. He was defrosting some chicken.

"Sure, we would love to stay," Brett answered as he smiled at me.

I was disgusted. I backed away further away from them, trying to act as normal as I could.

"What are you making for supper?" I asked as I sat down at the table.

"Chicken and potatoes," Caleb answered as he took out some wine from the cupboards.

"So Caleb, when did our fine Liz arrive here?" Kevin asked as he poured himself a glass of wine.

"Earlier this evening. I'm so thrilled she has decided to be with me," Caleb answered. He came over and kissed my lips.

"I'm happy I came to my senses and convinced myself that I needed to be with you," I said as I tried not to puke.

The boys were talking about the usual: sex, blood, and whatever else. I was trying to ignore them. I needed to think of a way to get Caleb's blood without him finding out. I got up and went upstairs. I needed to text Hunter. I needed some ideas.

+ + +

"She sure is yummy," Kevin said.

"I know. Caleb, can you share?" Brett asked.

"Now, boys, behave. She is mine," Caleb answered as he put the chicken in the oven.

"Alright, we will try," Brett answered. He looked disappointed.

+ + +

I was upstairs texting Hunter. I needed to be quick so Caleb wouldn't find out. *How can I get Caleb's blood?* I asked him. I waited a few minutes to get a response. I finally got a message from Hunter. I went to open it when I heard footsteps outside the door. I panicked and put my phone under the bed. Just then the door opened and Caleb walked in.

"Are you alright?" Caleb asked, looking concerned.

"Not really. I don't feel well," I replied as I held onto my stomach.

"Is there anything I can do to help?" Caleb asked, stepping closer to me.

"Not really. I just need some time by myself," I replied, hoping he would get the hint and leave.

"Ok, but don't be too long. We are missing you," Caleb answered as he turned around and shut the door behind him. I waited a few minutes before getting my phone from underneath the bed.

"Let's see what Hunter said," I whispered to myself as I opened the message. It read *"You must take his blood when he is sleeping; hybrids are very hard sleepers. But you must be fast, and don't leave traces behind."*

I sighed and put my phone away so no one could find it. I waited a bit and then opened the door and headed for the stairs. I found all three of them sitting in the living room laughing and telling jokes. I shook my head and had a seat on the empty sofa by the window.

"There you are," Kevin said, smiling.

"Yep, here I am," I replied sarcastically.

"Don't mock me," Kevin snapped.

"I'm not. I simply just told you I was here," I said, smiling back at him.

"Ok, you two, cut it out," Caleb said.

I sat there in complete silence. I didn't want to talk to any of them, but I knew I had to be there in order to save Kelvin.

"I'm going to bed. Caleb, sweetie, would you like to join?" I asked. I went behind him and slid my hands down his chest and kissed his cheek.

"Sure, I would love to, baby," Caleb answered and jumped off the couch.

"I would love to join," Kevin said.

"Me too," Brett replied as he watched me and licked his lips.

Upstairs, Caleb and I undressed each other. I tossed him on the bed, landed on top of him and we had sex. Afterwards, he fell asleep almost instantly. I looked around the room and then grabbed a pill bottle that I found in the bathroom. I went up to Caleb and poked his finger with a needle. It bled a lot. I put the pill bottle under his finger and watched the blood dribble into the bottle. I filled it almost to the top and put the lid back on. I put the bottle in my purse and grabbed my phone to put in my purse so I wouldn't forget it. I crawled back into bed and dozed off. The next morning I woke up to the smell of bacon. I got up and headed for the washroom, where I got cleaned up. I headed downstairs, still in my nightgown.

"Good morning, sleeping beauty," Caleb said as he kissed my lips.

"Good morning," I replied. I got myself a cup of coffee. "Say, did Brett and Kevin spend the night?" I asked as I poured milk into my coffee and stirred it.

"No, they were gone when I got up this morning," Caleb answered. He stood beside me staring at me.

"Oh, just wondering. They are creepy," I said. "Why are you staring at me?" I asked. I looked at him and backed away.

"Honey, I know what you did to me last night. That was very bad of you," Caleb snapped as he hung on to me.

"I don't know what you're talking about," I hissed. I shoved him into the wall and ran upstairs. I opened the door, ran to my purse, pulled my cell out and quickly texted Hunter "112." I looked around the room to see where I could hide— who I was I kidding, he could smell me. The door swung open and I stood there waiting for him to beat me.

"You almost had me convinced that you were all mine," Caleb snarled as he tossed me on the bed.

I lay on the bed. I knew I needed to think of a spell that would act fast. I shouted *capitis dolorem* and Caleb dropped to the floor holding his head in pain. I took this opportunity to jump off the bed and run off before he had a chance to do anything. I ran out of the room and down the stairs, but Brett and Kevin were blocking the door way.

"Where do you think you're going, missy?" Kevin asked as he held onto my arm. I turned around and bit him. Kevin screamed in pain. He let me go as he dropped to the floor holding his arm.

"You little bitch," Brett snapped as he pulled out a sliver knife. Just before he was about to stab me there was crash through the front door.

"What the fuck," Brett said as we all backed up.

"Hunter!" I said.

"I got your text," Hunter said, smiling.

Caleb came running downstairs. He was extremely pissed off, and he started to shift. I just stood there, as I was too weak to shift. I hadn't had blood in days. Hunter looked at me as he held on to his head. I noticed something different about him. Was Hunter turning into a hybrid?

Chapter 3

HUNTER'S IDENTITY

Hunter suddenly looked up, and his eyes turned red. He started growling at Caleb. Caleb growled back as he came closer towards me. He was just about to leap at me when I raised my hand and threw him against the wall. Hunter started to shift into a werewolf. I couldn't believe it! He looked exactly like me, but he was black. Hunter and Caleb stood there growling until Caleb leaped at Hunter. Hunter stepped out of the way and grabbed Caleb, chucking him against the wall. The wall started to crack. Caleb just lay there for a few seconds. He shook his head and stood back up. I needed to do something fast. I needed to feed. I looked at Kevin, and he was standing there cheering Caleb on. I moved really fast behind him and bit into his neck. He struggled to get away, but I was too strong. Brett grabbed me and tossed me off Kevin.

"You bitch! What did you do?" Brett asked as he checked to see if Kevin was still alive.

"I got my strength back," I said, laughing.

In the meantime, Caleb and Hunter stood there staring at each other. Caleb started growling and he leaped at Hunter, throwing Hunter into the window. Glass smashed everywhere. Caleb pinned Hunter down so Brett could run over and stab Hunter with a silver knife I saw him dig one out of the kitchen drawer. I chanted a few words and Brett fell down in pain, which gave me enough time to shift. I shifted into my wolf form and lunged at Caleb, knocking him off Hunter. Hunter stood up and we surrounded Caleb. Caleb gave up and shifted back into human form, and so did we. We stood there trying to catch our breath. I glared at Caleb.

"I will get Liz once and for all, when you are least expecting it," Caleb snarled as he walked past us.

I already had my purse downstairs in a secret area so I could grab it and go. I went to get it and Hunter and I left.

"Come on, Liz, this way," Hunter said as we ran down the back alley. There was a car up ahead.

"Hunter, we're naked," I commented as we stopped at the car. The window rolled down and it was Damien.

"Hop in, you two," Damien demanded as Hunter opened the door and we both got in.

"Well, isn't this awkward… seeing that we are brother and sister and we are both naked," I said. I felt really embarrassed.

"I know, Liz, but we had to do what needed to be done," Hunter replied as he smiled at me.

"Thank god you are ok," Damien said.

"Yeah, I know, that was a close call," I said as I took a deep breath.

We made it home. Hunter and I ran in and got a change of clothing while Damien brought my mother Caleb's blood.

"Thanks, Damien," Jane said as he poured the blood into a bowl.

I came running downstairs and everyone was scattered throughout the living room.

"Hey honey, I need you to help me with this spell," my mother said as she held onto my hand.

I looked at Kelvin. He was so still. I missed him so much. I squeezed my mom's hand as I started to cry.

"Aw, honey, I know you miss him, but I need you to be strong for me, ok?" my mother said as she wiped the tears off my face. I looked at her and nodded.

She took the blood and put some on Kelvin's face, chest, and arms. We both started chanting over and over again; it was such a strong spell that our lights started blinking and our belongings started flying off the walls and shelves. We just kept chanting until everything stopped and our lights went completely out. We stopped. I stared at Kelvin. Nothing was happening. I was getting worried that this spell was a waste of time and I slept with Caleb for nothing. I got up and ran upstairs, lay on my bed and started crying. Celina was looking at me through her crib.

"Mama," Celina said.

"Celina, did you call me mama?" I asked in excitement.

Celina just looked at me and smiled. She jumped up and down as she started laughing. I smiled and grabbed her out of the crib and kissed her.

+ + +

"I don't think it worked, Jane," Blair said as he looked at Kelvin.

"I don't understand. I did everything I was supposed to," Jane said as she read the spell over again.

Just then, Kelvin opened his eyes and started coughing. He slowly got up and covered his eyes. "What happened to me?" he asked as he tried to open his eyes.

"Caleb bit you and you died," Jane explained. "I found a spell that would bring you back, but that involved Liz pretending to want to be with Caleb so she could steal his blood. That is how much she loves you." She hugged Kelvin.

"I don't know what to say. Where is Liz?" Kelvin asked as he stood up.

"She is upstairs crying," Jane replied.

+ + +

I came running downstairs with Celina in my arms. "Guess what? Celina called me mama!" I shouted in happiness. I looked over and saw Kelvin standing there. I rubbed my eyes to make sure he was real and he was. "Kelvin, I missed you so much. I will never let anything happen to you again," I said as I handed Celina over to Jane. I ran up to Kelvin and hugged him so tight. I never wanted to let go.

"Liz, thank you for saving my life. Now, Jane, if you can take care of Celina for a while, I have something I would like to take care of," Kelvin said, smiling as he carried me upstairs. He tossed me on the bed and crawled on top of me.

"You're welcome, baby," I replied as I kissed him.

Kelvin pulled down his pants as he kissed me. I pulled mine down and he inserted himself into me. I started moaning like crazy. It felt so good I scratched his back and he groaned a bit too. He started to slow down as he moaned. He lay on top of me for a bit and we kissed some more.

"I missed you so much," I said as I looked at him.

"I'm sorry I got in the way," Kelvin said as he rolled off me.

"Don't be sorry. You were trying to help," I replied. I turned to face him.

"I know, but I caused you so much grief," Kelvin said. He pulled my hair away from my face.

I just looked at him and smiled. I couldn't believe he was back. I swore to myself I would never let anything like this happen again. Kelvin was soon sound asleep. I couldn't sleep, so I went downstairs to see if anyone was awake. I just saw Hunter and my mother sitting on the couch watching TV, so I went to join them.

"Hello. I can't sleep," I said as I sat down on the sofa next to Hunter.

"How is Kelvin?" my mother asked.

"He's good. He's sleeping," I replied.

"Liz, there is something I need to tell you. Kelvin is now a hybrid. Usually you can't create hybrids that way, but in order to bring him back to life, the spell we did turned him into a one," my mother explained.

"Ok, well, that doesn't bother me. I am a hybrid and so is Celina," I said, shrugging my shoulders.

"I know, honey, but I don't know how he is going to respond to it. The transformation could really affect him in such a way that he may never turn back into human form," my mother explained with a serious look.

"Alright, well, what am I supposed to do?" I asked.

"I don't know. I am working on that part," my mother replied.

I just sighed. I was getting so frustrated. Why couldn't anything work out? There always had to be something.

"Liz, everything will work out," Hunter said.

"I wish I could think that way. It seems as soon as something gets fixed, another problem occurs. I can't win," I snarled as I stood up and went into the kitchen to grab something to drink.

+ + +

"Poor girl. She has gone through so much," Hunter said to our mother.

"I know, but believe it or not she has turned into a beautiful strong woman," Jane said.

"I know she has," Hunter agreed.

+ + +

"You guys, I am going for a walk. I need some fresh air," I said as I got my shoes on and grabbed a jacket. I opened the door and headed outside.

"Wait, Liz," Hunter shouted as he got his shoes and jacket on and came running after me.

"Why can't I be by myself?" I asked as I crossed my arms.

"You know why," Hunter replied.

"Yeah, I know, but sometimes I need time to think," I replied as I took off the other way.

"Liz, wait, stop!" Hunter shouted as he took off after me. I could hear him running and calling my name but I wanted to be myself so bad. I turned the corner and watched Hunter run past me. He soon stopped and came down the path to where I was.

I rolled my eyes. "I forgot you can sense where I am," I said, pouting.

"Don't do that ever again, do you hear me?" Hunter snapped as he held onto my wrist.

"Yes, big brother, you don't have to get so angry," I snarled as I moved away. We stepped back onto the street and it started to rain. I was talking to Hunter when all of a sudden Hunter dropped to the ground. I looked around; there was no one around us. I bent down to see if I could wake Hunter up, and I noticed some tranquilizer darts in his back. I got up quickly and started smelling around me to see if I could sense anything. I looked up at one of the buildings and saw a man up there.

"Hey you, come down here!" I yelled.

I got no response. I was starting to get pissed off. I turned to look at Hunter and when I looked back where that man had been, he was gone. "What the hell is going on?" I asked myself. I turned around and there was a man standing there. I couldn't smell werewolf or vampire.

"What is going on?" I asked as I went up to him.

He still didn't say. He grabbed me, threw me up against one of the buildings and started patting me down. I turned around and grabbed him by his throat. My eyes turned red and I started growling. He had no expression. I dropped him on the ground and stared at him for a few seconds.

The man got up and started to cough, and then he cleared his throat. "I wouldn't have done that if I were you, little girl," he stated as he started to laugh.

I looked at him, confused. There was a helicopter above me and about five huge trucks circled Hunter and I. A lot of men jumped out— too many to count—and they all had guns. A couple men came over, picked Hunter up and threw him into the back of one of the trucks. Another man came over and handcuffed me and then held my shoulder and threw me in the passenger side of another truck. I could have easily escaped, but I wanted to toy around with them a bit. I was freezing. I couldn't stop shivering, and the rain was coming down hard.

"So what is your name?" the man asked as he tried to look at me while driving.

"Why do you want to know that? And what the hell is going on? What did me and my brother do?" I asked as I glared at him. His face was covered by a black ski mask, so he obviously didn't want me to see him, and by the way he gripped the steering wheel I could tell he was losing patience with me.

"I know you are angry and scared, but I will tell you everything when we get back to our base," the man said as he put his hand on my leg. I moved away. I didn't know what he was trying to pull, but I didn't like it.

"You are a little bitch, aren't you," he said. He pulled over to the side of the road and got a syringe out.

"What are you doing?" I asked.

"Giving you something so you will cooperate with me, honey," the man said, and he grabbed my arm and jabbed the syringe into it.

"What do you mean, cooperate?" I asked, confused.

"This solution is so you can't try anything stupid," he said. Then he got on top of me and started running his hand over my body. I was getting too weak. He was just about to rape me when his walkie-talkie went off.

"Are you there, Evan?" a voice asked.

"What awesome timing. I was going to get a piece of this sexy hybrid bitch," Evan mumbled to himself as he got off me and picked up his walkie-talkie. "Yes, Nathan. I am here."

"Where are you?" Nathan asked.

"I'm on my way," Evan replied as he started up his truck.

"Hurry, we need our girl," Nathan hissed.

"Yeah, yeah, don't we all," Evan mumbled to himself as he looked at me. I just stared out the window. I was disgusted. I didn't want to look at him right now. It felt like a long drive; it was so silent, and the rain never stopped. We turned down a dirt road and up ahead I saw a huge white building with lights everywhere. Evan parked the truck with the others in the parking lot, hopped out of the driver's side and opened the passenger's side. He threw me out and I landed in some mud. I got up and tried wiping it off me.

"Come on, sweetheart," Evan said, and he grabbed my arm and dragged me inside the building. I looked around to see if I could spot Hunter.

+ + +

Meanwhile, back home…

"Hey, you guys, I noticed Liz wasn't beside me in the bed anymore," Kelvin stated as he sat down on the couch.

"We don't know where she is. She went for a walk. Hunter went with her and now we are kind of getting worried," Mark said with a concerned look.

"I'm trying to find a spell on my children so I can locate them," Jane said.

+ + +

"Well, you must be the hybrid," a man's voice called out.

"Wouldn't you like to know," I snarled at him. I looked him up and down. He was tall and broad. His brown eyes looked me over, and as he ran his hands through his short brown hair, I noticed a weird moon symbol tattoo on his forearm. I couldn't really get a good look at it, though.

"Baby, you are feisty," the man said as he backhanded me.

"Yes. I am the hybrid. Why do you ask if you know?" I snapped.

"Just making sure we have the right chick. By the way, I am Mickey," Mickey stated as he observed me.

"Well, Mickey, I am letting you know you will not get away with this," I hissed as I shoved him.

"Yes we will, honey. Do you have any idea who we are?" Mickey shouted as he grabbed my hair and tossed me onto the floor.

They took off their masks and revealed what they looked like.

"I am Evan, honey. You met me earlier back in the truck," Evan smirked at me. His baby blue eyes stared at me, and he had long curly hair that sat on his shoulders. He was shorter than Mickey and stocky. "This, my friend, is Nathan," Evan pointed.

Nathan smiled and walked towards me. He kneeled down beside me. His cold hands touched my face. I looked at his green eyes and growled in disgust. He laughed a bit, and his breath smelled like garlic. It was enough to make me puke. I tried to move over, but he held on to me. He brushed his face up to mine, and when his red beard brushed up against my cheek I noticed the same tattoo on Mickey, only Nathan's tattoo was on his neck. Nathan scratched his short red hair. He then whispered in my ear, "Sucks to be you, honey." He stood up and chuckled.

"You don't know what I am capable of," I snapped as my eyes turned purple.

"Yes, honey, we do. We have been watching you for some time now. Amazing, I must say at the least— you are gorgeous. We both wonder what it would be like to sleep with a hybrid," Mickey said as he smiled at me.

"I am flattered, but you are not getting anywhere with me," I snapped. I started to feel faint.

"Is that so, honey?" Mickey said as he watched me fall to the floor.

"What should we do with her?" Evan asked as he licked his lips.

"I know what I am doing with her," Mickey answered as he got on top of me and raped me.

I woke up a few hours later. I was all caged up, and I felt so dizzy and hungry. I looked around. There was no light, and it smelled like dust. It was so cold in this cage I could barely stand it. I heard footsteps and a few minutes later someone used a key and my cage door flew open.

"Get up, honey," Mickey said as he lifted me up by my arm.

"Ouch, that hurts," I snapped as I walked in front of him.

"You sure have a nice ass," Mickey stated as he grabbed my ass.

"Don't touch me," I snarled, and I shoved him aside.

"Don't be like that, sweetheart," Mickey replied as he laughed a bit and brought me into the main area of the building. The lights were dim and there was guards everywhere. I saw Hunter on the other side, and he didn't look well. They brought me closer to him and suddenly there was a loud bang and some bars came down around Hunter and I. We were locked up in a cage together and there was no way out.

"Now, you two, we need a show! Shift and fight each other," Mickey demanded.

"Are you out of your fucking mind? He is my brother," I growled.

"We are too weak!" Hunter growled

"You two are very demanding. Nathan, go bring them some blood," Mickey demanded.

Nathan soon approached us with one vial of blood each. We downed them.

"Thanks, but I refuse to fight my own brother," I snarled.

"Well, honey, you have no choice— if you refuse, then you and your brother get tormented even more," Mickey replied, laughing.

"Liz, we have to do this, and then we can think of a way to get out," Hunter said as he started to shift.

I stood there staring at Hunter. I couldn't shift. I was too scared. I didn't want to fight him. Hunter growled as he leaped at me, and I went flying into the bars. I slowly got up and looked at him. I started to shift, and we lunged at each other. Soon there was blood everywhere. Both of us started slowing down, as we were getting too weak, and finally we both collapsed. Hunter and I woke up a few minutes later tied to chairs. I looked around and saw Mickey and Evan standing there.

"You two put up a good fight, I must say," Evan said as he came towards us.

I found something sharp that I used to cut myself free, and I acted as if nothing happened. I stood up, flew at Mickey and bit down on his neck and fed. He screamed for Evan to do something. Evan grabbed a taser and used it on me.

I fell to the floor in pain, and I still felt hungry. I looked at Hunter; he looked so weak.

"You stupid bitch. You should be punished," Evan snapped as he kicked my side.

Mickey slowly got up, holding his neck. He grabbed a cloth and wrapped it around his neck. "Get up!" he yelled at me.

I slowly got up and stared at him. He backhanded me. I was fed up with this shit, and I turned around slowly. My eyes were purple, and I started to growl. I could feel my adrenalin pump through my veins. I started to shift into a werewolf again, and I went over to Hunter set him free.

"Holy fuck, Mickey, let's go!" Evan shouted as he ran towards the door. I noticed him run and I lunged at the door, trapping him inside the room. Hunter slowly stood up and bit Evan's neck, and Evan fell to the floor screaming. Hunter shifted into a werewolf too, and I could hear Mickey on his walkie-talkie.

"Guys, the two hybrids have shifted, and they are on the loose!" Mickey shouted into his device.

Mickey could hear screams and gunshots coming from outside. Hunter and I shifted back into our human form and knocked a couple guards out. We stole their clothing, jumped the fence and headed out into the field.

"Liz, this was your fault. If you didn't go for that walk then we would be home," Hunter said as he stormed away.

I stood there in shock. He was right— it was my fault. What had I done?

"You're right. I am sorry. I didn't know," I replied as I walked faster to catch up to him.

Hunter and I found a spot in the forest to sleep for the night. I was so cold lying there, and I couldn't keep myself warm. Hunter lay down behind me and snuggled up to me.

"Liz, don't get any wrong ideas. I am only doing this because you're cold," Hunter stated.

"I know. I'm not. Don't worry," I replied as I backed up closer to him.

"You are getting too close," Hunter said.

"What do you mean, too close?" I asked as I turned to face him.

"What I mean is, you are my sister, and you are invading my space. If you weren't my sister I would be all over you," Hunter explained as he smiled.

I chuckled a bit and tried to fall asleep. It was hard when my mind was on overdrive. "Do you think we will ever be safe?" I asked softly.

"Hard to say. Now get some rest. We have a long day ahead of us tomorrow," Hunter said as he closed his eyes and began to yawn.

I sighed and tried to get comfortable. I was not used to sleeping on the ground, and I sure would rather be doing other things right then. Not fighting man-made hybrids and running from problems that didn't seem to go away, but just got worse.

The next morning the sun was shining in our face so we got up. I yawned and stretched, sitting on a stump as I waited for Hunter to wake up. Hunter finally got up, stretched and walked over to me.

"Come on, we have to get going. Those men are probably looking for us," Hunter stated.

"Alright," I said as I sighed a bit. I stood up and we started walking, hoping to find the road soon.

"I am sorry about yesterday. I felt like I was a little harsh on you," Hunter apologized.

"You had the right to say that it is my fault that we are in this situation. Dad was right. I have to stop running away from my problems. I find it so hard to break out of that habit. I grew up pretty much my whole life without anyone to turn to," I replied.

"I understand. But now you have a whole family that cares about you and loves you," Hunter said, smiling.

"I know. And I feel very lucky to have you guys in my life," I said, smiling back. "How am I going to tell Kelvin that he is a hybrid?"

"You're just going to have to be blunt with him," Hunter said.

"I guess there is no soft way in telling him," I replied. My legs were starting to hurt from walking so much.

+ + +

"Okay, guys, I am really starting to get worried," Kelvin said as he looked at the clock.

"I know. They have been gone for almost two days," Blair stated.

"I'm working on that spell. Just give me a few more minutes," Jane said as she took Liz's and Hunter's hair and put it in a bowl. She started chanting some words with her eyes closed then opened them suddenly.

"What is it, Jane?" Jeff asked.

"They were kidnapped from a government official then taken to their base about five hours away from Prince Albert. It looks like they escaped unharmed and they are trying to find their way back," Jane explained as she tried to communicate with Liz. She suddenly got a rush of visions and she dropped to the floor in pain.

"Jane, what is happening?" Mark asked as he helped her up.

"I just saw visions of those men coming back. They aren't too far behind them— in fact, they are catching up quickly. I need to get through to Hunter and Liz fast," Jane replied as she scrambled to figure out what to do.

+ + +

"Hunter, I smell humans," I said.

"I know, me too. Let's move faster," Hunter replied as we both started walking faster.

Hunter and I finally made it to the road. We kept walking. We wanted to make it to the nearest gas station to see how far Prince Albert was. We finally got to a gas station and we were asking for directions when we heard a voice calling out to us. We looked over to our right and there was a lady standing there flagging us down. We didn't know if we should go over there.

"Come on, guys, I will explain everything to you later. You don't have time," she said.

We followed her into a back room, and just as soon as we left we heard those men come crashing through the door. She handed us some old clothing that was lying around. Hunter put on some blue overalls, and I put on some black sweats and an oversized blue t-shirt.

"We know those two people came in here, we just seen them. Where did they go?" Mickey asked as he started throwing things off the shelves.

"Sir, calm down. What did they look like?" the clerk at the counter asked.

"The one was a petite, fine, young-looking lady with blonde long hair, and the other one was a young male, tall with black short hair," Mickey explained, sounding pissed off.

"Ok, yeah, I did see them. They went outside," the clerk replied.

"I don't know what these men want with us," I said as I looked around. The room we were in was small and there was shelf units everywhere.

"They want to do tests and make themselves into hybrids, and unfortunately for the girl, they want to mate with you after they are done with the experiment and everything goes well," the lady explained.

"Yuck, that is gross! How do you know so much, and what is your name?" I asked, disgusted.

"My name is Katie, and I have been in the base. I am just a vampire, but you, honey… you are special. They will stop at nothing to have you back. When I was kidnapped they did a lot of tests and raped me. I escaped, though," Katie explained as she dropped her red hood down so we could see her face. She was a petite young girl, maybe in her twenties, with red long hair. Her skin was covered in freckles. I looked into her blue eyes, and they were full of fear. She spoke with an English accent.

"That is horrible. They better not have touched my sister," Hunter snarled.

"Oh, don't worry. I have, and fuck, she is mmm… delicious," Mickey said.

"How did we not hear you come in?" Katie asked, looking pissed off.

"Oh my dear Katie. We have been doing a lot of tests, and I am turning into a hybrid so I can be sneaky now," Mickey explained as he looked at me and winked.

I looked at him, disgusted, and then looked away.

+ + +

"Did you get through to them?" Mark asked Jane.

"Shit. I was too late. They found them already, and they are in a gas station. The guy with them is a hybrid, too. This isn't good. He is going to want Liz," Jane replied, looking terrified.

"What? Why!" Kelvin shouted as he stood up.

"They are going to want to mate with her," Jane said.

"Fuck that. I am going after them," Kelvin snapped as he stood up, but he felt dizzy and fell back down.

"Kelvin, I need to explain something to you. When Liz and I brought you back to life, there was one down side. You are now a hybrid," Jane replied.

Chapter 4

EXPERIMENT GONE WRONG

"Well then, that will make me stronger so I can go help them," Kelvin said as he stood up slowly, holding his stomach.

"No. This hybrid that these humans are turning into… they are different. Much stronger," Jane stated.

"Well, we can't leave them," Tyler spoke up as he came out of the spare room.

"Tyler, did we wake you?" Blair asked.

"No, I heard everything. Is there anything Steven and I can do?" he asked as he rubbed his eyes and yawned.

"We are trying to come up with a plan, but we need to act fast," Jane answered.

+ + +

"So what, now you are going to kidnap us?" I asked.

"Honey, of course. And this time you won't escape," Mickey said as he came closer to me.

"Don't you touch her," Hunter shouted as he shoved Mickey out of the way and grabbed my hand. We went running out the back door, and they were right behind us.

"Hunter, what are we going to do?" I asked as we came to a complete stop. We were surrounded.

"You two hybrids don't fucking give up, do you?" Mickey snapped as he went to grab me. As soon as he touched me, he went flying backwards.

"What the…" I said as I touched my arm.

+ + +

"That should be good enough for now until they can make it home. I placed a spell on them that acts like a huge shield so no one can harm them," Jane said, smiling.

"You bitch. You sure have a lot of surprises up your sleeve," Mickey said as he got up, laughing.

"Yeah, well, you shouldn't fuck with a witch," I snarled.

"Oh, you're a witch. That is interesting," Mickey replied, looking shocked.

"My family is strong. We are one of a kind," I stated as I glared at him.

"I see that, but that doesn't mean I am letting you escape, dear," Mickey replied. He didn't look a bit scared.

Hunter and I held hands and started howling. We could hear other howling, and soon we were surrounded with werewolves. Mickey and Ethan just looked around. They started smiling— they weren't even scared.

"You guys think a bunch of werewolves are going to scare us? Ha, think again," Mickey snarled as him and Nathan started to shift into huge hybrids. They were all black with red eyes. They growled at the other werewolves and they backed off.

"Hunter, what the fuck are we going to do?" I asked, starting to get pissed off.

"I don't know," Hunter replied.

I glanced over past the other witch and I noticed a pack of wolves standing there. They looked like those wolves I saw back at that hotel with Damien, Hunter and the others. They stared at him, and the white one shifted into a woman. I was right; it was that pack. I stared back at her, and she was trying to communicate with me through her mind. I was able to hear her thoughts.

"We told you to come with us... now you must use all your powers," the wolf women stated.

"I don't know what you are talking about," I replied in my mind.

"You are very magical. Don't let them underestimate you," the wolf replied. I turned away for a couple seconds and looked over and they were gone. I stood there trying to figure out what she meant by that. The hybrids came after Hunter and I, and one swung at Hunter, sending him flying. The other hybrid was coming at me and I jumped over the monster. I broke off the necklace I was wearing and cast a spell on it. I stood there waiting for the hybrid to turn around, and just as he did I swung the necklace and stabbed the hybrid in his eye. He growled, and there was steam coming from his face. You could hear the burning of the necklace. I ran over to Hunter and helped him up, and as we started running we shifted into our hybrid forms. We could hear the other hybrids chasing us from a distance, but we never stopped. I got an idea: I stopped and turned back into a human, and Hunter did too.

"Liz, we don't have time," Hunter scowled.

"If we cast a spell to make our senses disappear, that will confuse them," I said as I started chanting some words. Hunter joined in. We didn't know if it worked, but we didn't want to stay around to find out either.

"Hunter, let's just shift into a regular wolf instead of a hybrid," I said.

"How do we do that?" Hunter asked, confused.

"Like this—just think about it," I said as I jumped and shifted into a white wolf.

"Alright," Hunter replied. He ran on all fours and soon he was a brown wolf.

We ran until we were surrounded by lights. We could smell vampires. We followed that sense and we started scratching the door of our home. It opened and we ran in. We quickly shifted back into humans and grabbed blankets to cover ourselves.

"What happened to you two?" Blair asked as he hugged us both.

"We were attacked by a government official. They took us back to their headquarters. They were doing some kind of experiment. I don't know how, but now they are both hybrids and very strong, I may add," I explained.

"That isn't good. They need to be stopped. How did you two escape?" Mark asked.

"I had a necklace on and I cast a spell upon it to turn it into silver. I stabbed one in the eye, then Hunter and I took off and we cast another spell so those hybrids would lose sense of us," I replied.

"I don't know how they will be stopped," Hunter stated.

"We are not sure, but there has to be someone that knows," Jeff said.

"At one point we called for help, but that didn't work. But there were these wolves… I saw them before. One shifted into a woman and we were communicating through our minds; she told me I was very magical and I needed to put a stop to these man-made creatures," I explained as I looked up at my mother. "Not to change the subject, but where is Kelvin?" I asked.

"He is having a shower," Tyler responded.

"Alright, anyways, I am going upstairs and getting in the shower too. Oh, and another thing— we ran into a vampire named Katie, and she told me they wanted to mate with me," I stated.

"Shit, that is not good," Mark replied.

"I will just make sure they don't figure out where I am," I said, shrugging my shoulders as I headed upstairs.

+ + +

Kelvin was done in the downstairs shower, and he stepped out of the washroom with a towel wrapped around his waist.

"Liz and Hunter are back safe and sound," Blair announced.

"Finally! I was getting worried. Where is Liz now?" Kelvin asked.

"She went upstairs to take a shower," Jane replied.

"Alright. I will go talk to her," Kelvin said as he headed upstairs.

+ + +

I went and checked up on Celina. She was getting so big. She must have already been a year old. She was lying there looking so adorable. I couldn't help but think she was going to have the same life I was living right now.

"Hey, honey," Kelvin said as he came and put his arm around my waist.

"Hey, honey," I replied as I kissed him.

"I am going to go jump in the shower. I will be back, baby," I said. I went into the washroom, got undressed and turned on the taps. The shower was so nice. I got dried off and dressed. I wiped the mirror off and stared into for a while. I sighed and put my hair back in a clip, opened the door and saw Hunter standing there talking to Kelvin.

"Is she alright?" Hunter asked.

"She seems to be a little distraught, but other than that I think she is alright. We didn't talk, really. She is in the shower," Kelvin replied.

"I don't know if I can continue to protect her. I love her, but it seems like she is always in danger and this last time was a close call. I mean, these man-made hybrids, they are very powerful and with Liz and I being pure blood and her being a witch and me being a wizard, things still didn't go right," Hunter explained as a tear ran down his cheek.

I stepped out of the washroom and spoke up. "Hunter, you don't have to take care of me. You have done enough for me, and you're right. No matter what, I am always in danger and now Celina will have to have the same life as me." I sat down on the edge of the bed.

"Liz ,it's not that I don't want to protect you. I am just saying I don't know if I can anymore. I mean, with Caleb wanting to have you and that diamond in his grasps, and those man-made hybrids wanting you as well, we are just not powerful enough," Hunter explained as he sat next to me.

"I understand. I just don't know what I am going to do, then," I said. I stood up and went downstairs. I walked in the living room and everyone went silent when I got there.

"Why is everyone silent?" I asked as I looked around.

"Honey, I am running out of options. We are going to have to send you away to the States. I have friends there. You are not safe here, and I won't be able to live with myself if anything happens to you," my dad explained as he hugged me.

"Ok… by myself? When?" I asked as I tried not to cry.

"Yes, by yourself for now. We were thinking of flying you out tomorrow," he explained.

"Ok. I don't know what else you can do. I will go get packed," I said. I went upstairs and got my bag out and started to pack.

"Liz, what are you doing?" Hunter and Kelvin asked me.

"I am being sent away to live with some of dad's friends in the States for now until things cool down," I replied as I zipped up my bag and kissed Celina goodbye.

"Mama," Celina replied.

"If you think that is for the best, we will be waiting for you and I will always love you," Kelvin said as he kissed me.

"I love you guys too, but I think I am going to sleep for a little bit," I said as I kissed Kelvin and hugged Hunter. I crawled into bed and I was out.

+ + +

"Hello, Tristan? It's Blair. Can my daughter come stay with you for a while? She needs a hideout," Blair asked.

"Yes, of course. I will get her bed made. Give her my number so I can pick her up at the airport," Tristan said.

"Yes, of course, and thank you," Blair said, and he hung up the phone.

+ + +

I woke up and looked at the time. It was 8:00 in the morning. I got up, grabbed my luggage and headed downstairs.

"Good morning. Are you ready?" Mark asked.

"I guess," I replied as I hugged everyone.

"Liz, keep in touch, dear," my mother said as she hugged me, and she handed me a necklace with three crescent moons.

"Thanks. I love it," I said as I waved goodbye.

Mark and I hopped in the car and took off.

"You must be scared," Mark said.

"A little, but I have to protect you guys too," I replied as I smiled at him.

We made it the airport. Mark helped me carry my luggage and he paid for my ticket. "Well, I guess this is it," he said, hugging me.

"Yeah, I guess so," I said as I hugged him back.

I started walking towards security. I looked at my ticket and it said Rapid City. I made it through security and tried to act as normal as I could. I didn't trust anyone. I found my seat one the plane, put my luggage away and sat down, looking out the window. About half an hour later the plane took off. I put in my headphones and fell asleep while listening to my music. I woke as we landed, with the pilot saying we had made it our destination. I texted Tristan that I was at the airport. I got my luggage and headed for the main part of the airport after going through all the security. I had no idea who I was looking for.

"Excuse me, ma'am, are you Liz?" a man asked me.

"Yes, I am," I replied. He was tall and well-built with a brown goatee, brown short, curly hair, and his arms were covered in tattoos. I glanced at his brown eyes and smiled.

"I am Tristan," he said as he shook my hand.

"Nice to meet you," I said. I felt kind of shy.

"You too, dear. Follow me. I parked out here," Tristan said as he pointed out to a limo. A gentleman opened the door for us and we crawled in the back.

"So what sort of troubles were you in?" Tristan asked.

"Where do I begin? There is this male hybrid named Caleb and he tried kidnapping me. He wants me to be his wife, and these man-made hybrids kidnapped my brother and I. They want me so they can mate with me, but these hybrids are so powerful," I explained.

"Wow, that is a lot for a young girl to take on," Tristan stated.

"I know, plus I have a little girl too. Her name is Celina," I said.

"No wonder your father wanted you safe. Well, you are safe with me, sweetie," Tristan said.

We soon turned into a narrow driveway. His house was amazing. It was huge, with a four-car garage, an outdoor swimming pool, a hot tub and a mini bar. "Wow! I am going to love it here," I said, smiling. We got out and I looked around. The pool was massive. I couldn't wait to try it. I followed him inside, took off my shoes and explored.

"Dear, I will show you around later. For now, come in and eat something," Tristan suggested.

"Alright," I said as I went into the kitchen. The hallway was covered in vine plants and different paintings, and there were three floors and an elevator. The kitchen had a huge stainless steel fridge and an island, and he had a saltwater tank built into the wall. He brought me a glass of blood and some steak. I couldn't believe my eyes. "Thank you so much," I said as I inhaled my drink and ate my steak.

"You sure were hungry," Tristan said, laughing. He took my dishes over to the sink.

"Yeah, I guess I was," I replied as I wiped the food of my face.

"Follow me into the living room. I will introduce you to my friends," Tristan said.

I got up and followed him there.

"Hey guys, please pay attention to me. I have someone I would like you to meet," Tristan demanded. "Liz, this is Cassidy. The one sitting by the fireplace is Mike, and last but not least the man sitting over by the piano is Darren." Tristan pointed them out to me. I studied all three of them. Cassidy's long blonde hair flowed down her back. She looked up at me with her green eyes. She had tattoos on her arms and legs too. She was wearing a beautiful red dress that stopped at her knees. She smiled at me. Her red lipstick made her white teeth stand out even more. Mike had one brown eye and one green eye. I didn't stare, as I didn't want to be rude. He had a multi-coloured mohawk and his left earlobe was pierced. He had a few tattoos on his arms, but not as many as the other two. Darren was bald. His dark-blue eyes glanced over at me and I noticed a scar above his right eye. He had a brown chinstrap.

"Hello, nice to meet you guys," I replied, waving.

"What is she? I can't smell her," Darren asked. He stood up. He was shorter, for a guy, and very muscular. His arms were huge, and he walked over and sniffed me.

"Darren, stop acting like an idiot. You can so smell her," Tristan snapped.

"I know. I am just fooling around. Welcome home, our little hybrid," Darren said, laughing a bit.

"Thanks, I guess. Where is my room so I can put my luggage away?" I asked as I picked up my suitcases.

"Follow me," Tristan said. He went upstairs and took me to the farthest room on the right. The room was nice; it has a big, king-size bed and an attached bathroom with a Jacuzzi.

"Wow, thanks," I said. I placed my luggage on the bed and it moved around. "Cool, a waterbed!" I said joyfully.

"Yes, Liz, this is your room and you can stay here as long as you need to," Tristan said, and he left the room. I closed the door as soon as he was gone. I got unpacked and changed into a nice dress. I put on the necklace my mother gave me and went downstairs.

"Liz, you look amazing," Tristan said as he greeted me at the bottom of the stairs.

"Thanks. I am not wearing anything too fancy— just figured I should dress a little nicer," I replied, blushing.

"Let's go out tonight to a club," Tristan said.

"I am not a huge drinker, but I will have a few," I replied.

"Alright, but I am doing Liz's hair and makeup," Cassidy said, smiling. We ran upstairs.

+ + +

"What do you think of her?" Mike asked Tristan.

"I think she is one of a kind. She is gorgeous, smart, funny, brave, outgoing, her heart is in the right place— she needs some guidance, though," Tristan replied as he drank the rest of his blood.

"Did you expect Blair to call you and ask you to take care of his daughter?" Darren asked.

"No. I knew he had a daughter, but I didn't know they reunited with each other. She has her mother's looks," Tristan said as he went into the kitchen to put his cup in the sink.

+ + +

"I think Tristan likes you. Actually, I know he is going to really care about you," Cassidy stated as she curled my hair.

"How can you tell he likes me?" I asked.

"The way he acts around you. The way he stares at you. When Blair asked him to take care of you, he didn't think twice about it. He has known Blair and Jane for a long time," Cassidy explained as she put hairspray in my hair.

"I already really like it here, but I do miss my family back home," I replied, smiling at her.

"I know, honey, and you will. No one expects you to leave them behind. Now let's go downstairs," Cassidy said.

I went into the kitchen where Tristan was. I opened the fridge and poured some blood into a glass. I held it up to my mouth and turned around and Tristan was staring at me, so I put the glass down and just waited for him to say something.

"Are you alright, Tristan? Is there something wrong with my hair? You're staring at me like there is something wrong with me." I looked at him funny.

"No, not at all. It's just that you look like your mother," Tristan replied.

"Did you get along with her?" I asked.

"Yes, all three of us hung out all the time, and then we just grew apart," Tristan. His phone rang and he took it out of his pocket and answered it. "Hello?" It must have been my family, because Tristan said, "Yes, she is right here did you want to talk to her?"

"Hello?" I answered.

"Hello, dear. It's your father. How was your trip? How is everything going?"

"Great. Everything is wonderful. Don't worry about me," I said ecstatically.

"Alright, well, phone if you need anything or if you just want to talk. Love you," my father replied, laughing.

"Love you too," I said, hanging up.

"Alright, are we ready to go?" Tristan asked us.

"Yeah, we are," we all replied.

We got on our shoes and headed out the door. The weather wasn't too bad: a little windy, but nothing terrible. We got in the limo and drove to the nearest nightclub. There was a huge lineup and a lot of lights. We parked our limo and piled out. I felt a little bit out of place, but I was going to try and have some fun. We walked to the back of the line, which was all humans. I could smell them.

"Tristan, this is a huge lineup and I am hungry," I complained as I held onto my stomach.

"I know, dear, we will be in soon. I could get us in sooner, but I don't want to bring attention to us, and as far as you being hungry, that will have to wait…" Tristan looked across the street as something caught his attention.

"What is it?" I asked. I looked over, and there was a tall man dressed all in black. We looked at each other, then when I looked back and he was gone. Tristan and I looked back at each other and shrugged our shoulders.

"Do you guys have ID?" the security man asked us.

We showed him our ID and walked in. The music and the people were very loud, and the smell was overwhelming. I could smell blood.

"Tristan, I don't like this place. I am having a hard time controlling myself," I said.

"I know, but this is the best place to come to overcome your instincts and try and control yourself," Tristan replied. He went over to the bar and bought two drinks, and then walked towards me and handed me one.

"Thanks, but what is it?" I asked. I smelled it and turned my face away in disgust.

"It's the vodka special. Try it," Tristan said, laughing.

I stared at it for a few seconds and finally tried it. "It is pretty good," I said as I sipped on it.

"Told you, Anyway, let's go join the others," Tristan said. I followed him to where Cassidy, Darren, and Mike were hanging out.

I started pounding my drinks back. I had never been drunk before, but I didn't have a care in the world at this point, as noone knew I was there. "Hey Tristan, you're kind of cute," I said as I stumbled towards him.

"Thanks, but Liz, you are drunk," Tristan said, laughing as he hung on to me.

"No, I am not. I'm sober!" I replied, laughing hysterically.

I hung on to Tristan and looked up, kissed his lips then fell down laughing.

"Alright, honey, let's take you home," Tristan said as he picked me up.

All of a sudden there were screams coming from outside, and the others were nowhere to be seen. Tristan grabbed me and brought me outside. We saw Darren feeding on a human right in front of people. Mike and Cassidy went up to Tristan and brought me to the limo while Tristan went up to Darren.

"What the fuck are you doing? Let's go. This is forbidden!" Tristan shouted as he grabbed Darren and threw him into the limo. Tristan got in and slammed the door. "Drive," he demanded to the driver.

"What happened?" I asked. I could barely even see straight.

"Nothing, Liz," Tristan answered.

"Wow…everything is spinning, and I feel like dancing," I said. I tried getting up, but Tristan hung on to me.

"Sit down, sweetie," Tristan demanded.

"You're not fun," I said. I pouted and then I turned to him. "Hey, would you fuck me?" I asked as I ran my fingers up and down his chest.

"No, you are my best friend's daughter," Tristan said, moving over.

"Fine," I said, and crossed my arms.

We finally made it back home and Tristan carried me inside and brought me upstairs. He lay me on the bed, left and shut the door. I got up and opened the door, went downstairs and sat on the couch.

"Liz, I put you on your bed for a reason. Now please, get some rest," Tristan said.

"I'm thirsty," I said. As I stood up, my eyes went red.

"Alright. I will get you something to drink," Tristan said as he brought me a glass of blood.

I took it from him and drank all of it. I wiped my mouth and handed him glass. "Thanks. Now I will go to bed," I said. I wandered upstairs, got undressed and got into my blue silky nightgown. I was stumbling everywhere. I collapsed on my bed and I was out.

+ + +

"Good night, sweet dreams," Tristan said after Liz left.

"You really care about her, don't you?" Cassidy asked.

"Yes, I do. Now if you will excuse me, I am going to get some rest too," Tristan said, and he went upstairs.

+ + +

I woke up to birds singing and the sun shining in my face. I slowly got up and rubbed my head. I got undressed and jumped in the shower. I could barely stand straight. I was still feeling drunk as I stood there while the water poured down my frail body. I finally turned off the taps and dried off. I put on my nightgown, dried my hair, braided it then crawled back into bed. I woke up to the sun shining right in my face again and I jumped out of bed and looked around. I almost forgot where I was. I had a bit of headache, but nothing to major. I went the washroom and washed my face. When I took my braid out, my hair was all wavy. I smiled at myself in the mirror and went out of my room. As I was going downstairs I could see Tristan talking to someone at the door. I didn't get a good look, but I was sure the man saw me because Tristan turned his head and saw me there. He closed the door.

"Who was that?" I asked as I went into the kitchen.

"No one important. Anyways, how are you feeling?" Tristan asked as he turned the burners on.

"Good. I have a bit of a headache," I replied, looking through the newspaper.

"That is good, considering you got drunk out of your mind, you were falling all over the place and laughing, and at one point you asked me if I would fuck you," Tristan replied.

"Umm ok… I don't know why I would ask that. I feel embarrassed," I said as I scratched my head.

"Don't be. You were drunk. Anyway, I told you no," Tristan answered as he pulled the bacon apart.

"Oh," I said, a little disappointed.

"You sound disappointed... like I couldn't resist you," Tristan replied. The bacon sizzled on the pan as he placed it down.

"No. I am not disappointed. I guess I am used to guys drooling over me," I replied.

"Well, I am not going to lie, you are very attractive and you being part witch, vampire, and lycanthrope... I mean, it's tough, but I promised Blair I would take care of you," Tristan explained as he cracked some eggs and put them into a separate pan.

"Fair enough. It's just when the full moon hits, my libido gets crazy and I might not be able to handle it," I admitted, embarrassed.

"Really? The next full moon is tomorrow night," Tristan said, looking at me.

"Yep. So I might not be able to control my hormones," I said. I got up and walked towards him. I whispered in his ear, "So if you really don't want me, then it is your loss." I caressed his chest and gently kissed his lips. He grabbed me and slammed me against the fridge, knocking everything off the top. He picked me up and put me on top of the counter, kissing me. His hands were all over me, and I started moaning. He pulled down his boxers and inserted himself into me. He fucked me hard, and after a few minutes he finished with a loud moan. He pulled his boxers up and I sat there for a bit, smiling at him.

"Wow," Tristan said as he wiped the sweat off my face. He felt my chest up some more.

"You are so sexy," I said as I pushed my body into him.

"Are you still horny?" Tristan asked, kissing me.

"A little bit," I replied as I bit my bottom lip.

"You are a wild girl," Tristan said as he finished making breakfast.

I giggled and jumped off the counter. I sat back down at the table and Cassidy, Mike, and Darren walked in and sat at the table as well.

"Breakfast is ready. Come help yourselves," Tristan said as he winked at me.

We all filled our plates and sat back down. Everyone was silent. I finished eating and put my dishes in the sink, then went upstairs and jumped in the shower. I was enjoying my shower when I opened my eyes and Tristan was standing there.

"You scared me," I said.

"Sorry. Man, I can't get enough of you—what did you do to me?" Tristan said as he came over to me. He dragged me out of the shower and tossed me on the bed.

"I swore to Blair I wouldn't sleep with you. I can't figure out what makes you irresistible. I have seen a lot of hot girls, but man, I can't resist you. Why is that?" Tristan said, sounding frustrated.

"I am the only female hybrid. I am very powerful and there is a scent that I give off," I explained as I stood up and put my housecoat on. Tristan just stared at me, watching my every move.

"How come Darren and Mike don't make any moves on you?" Tristan asked.

"I don't know," I said as I sat down at the edge of the bed.

Tristan was about to step closer to me when there was a knock at the door. We both got up and went downstairs. Tristan opened the door and there stood a tall, slim man. He looked like the one we saw at the club. He was wearing a brown trench jacket and a brown hat. He kept trying to hide his face in his jacket.

"Hello. May I come in?" he asked as he stepped inside. He had a deep, crackly voice.

"I guess so. Who are you and what do you want?" Tristan asked as he shut the door behind him.

"You must be Liz," the strange man said as he held my hand. "You are in danger. You must come with me. I have no time to explain."

"No! Let go of me!" I shouted as I pulled away.

"These vampires are not be trusted," the man said as he grabbed me and tossed me to another man. The other man was shorter, but very strong. His hands held on to me tightly.

"Let her go!" Tristan yelled.

I started yelling too, and everyone went down on their knees. They were all holding their heads, and I stopped.

"Ok, now that I have everyone's attention, here's what is going to happen— I am not going anywhere until I find out what the fuck is going on!" I shouted as I walked back inside. I stood there waiting for everyone to stand up and start talking. Seriously, who did they think they were coming in here and trying to take me away? I was done with that bullshit.

Chapter 5

FIGHT OR FLIGHT

Slowly, they all started to stand up, looking at me in shock.

"What the hell just happened?" one man asked me.

"I am a witch. Now please start explaining yourself, or things will get dirty," I commanded.

"I can't tell you right now," the man said.

"So you want to play fine," I replied as I grabbed him and threw him inside.

"I can't tell you. I was just sent here to take you to my master," the man said.

"Well, someone wants to meet me. You know what, fine. I am done running. I will go with you," I said, grinning.

"Liz, no," Tristan said, taking my hand.

"I will be okay. Now let's go," I said as I hugged Tristan and left with the two men.

We walked a little way to a bridge nearby. There was a strange man standing there. "I see you brought my hybrid," he said as he reached out to grab me.

"No way. Don't touch me. I came on my own free will, and I am not your hybrid," I snapped as I quickly pulled away.

"My, my, you sure are a feisty little girl," the man said, smiling as he checked me over. His creepy brown eyes raped my body, his breath smelled like cigars and his teeth where stained with a yellow tinge. He was tall and slim, and he just stood there and smoked his cigar, studying me very hard. He scratched the stubble on his face.

I looked at him in complete disgust."Why does everyone want me? Can't I live my life? I was happy where I was," I snarled as I started walking away.

"Because, dear ,you are very special and I wanted to meet you for myself. Let me tell you, I am not disappointed," the man said as he followed me.

I turned around, stopped and looked at him. "Well, mister. You met me. Now please let me live my life," I growled.

"How rude of me… my name is Robert," he introduced himself.

"I feel much better now that I know your name. Not. I am leaving," I said, and I started walking away.

"Wait, please, I want to get to know you," Robert replied.

I just ignored him and kept on walking. I was truly amazed that he was not running after me. Usually I can't escape that easily… I thought maybe I should just start agreeing and going with them instead of putting up a fight. When I finally made it back to Tristan's place, I was exhausted. I opened the door and heard Tristan talking to someone.

"Tristan, I'm back," I said. I shut the door, took my shoes off and stepped into the kitchen. I couldn't believe my eyes— there stood Caleb. I froze. I could feel anxiety building up, and I started shaking.

"Hello, baby, I didn't expect you back," Tristan said as he came over to me and held onto my arm.

Was this really happening? Was Caleb standing there, and was Tristan really talking to him? I thought I was here to escape, but all I could think was that he was going to kill me for standing him up.

"Well, dear, you are so easy to find," Caleb said. He came towards me and stabbed me in the stomach with a knife. I screamed and fell to the floor, crying. I put my hand over my wound and just stayed crouched down before looking up at them, my eyes overflowed with tears.

"I am sorry, honey, but that is what you get for making me look like a fool," Caleb said as he lifted me up by my hair and looked at me. He took the knife and slid it down my face. "You are too sexy to kill right now. My god, you are the only other female hybrid— I can't lose you." He smelled my hair.

"I am sorry, but you killed my boyfriend. I needed to get your blood and I knew you wouldn't hand it over. You're heartless." I spit in his face.

He wiped the spit off and slapped me across the face, and then grabbed me and pinned me up against the wall. "Tristan, hold her. I will be right back," Caleb demanded. Tristan took over and Caleb went upstairs.

"Tristan, how can you do this to me?" I asked as I tried squirming away.

"I planned this with Caleb the whole time, honey," Tristan said as he pushed himself into me.

"You are a monster. Wait until my family find out," I snapped as I bit his hand.

"You bitch. Ha, you think that will let you go?" Tristan snarled as he felt me up. "Fuck, you are a turn on. I don't know how I resisted you for so long."

Caleb came back downstairs and shoved Tristan aside. Flipping me over so I was facing him, he looked me up and down and licked his lips. "I will have you as my wife," Caleb stated as he threw me outside.

"Never! I will die before I become your wife!" I shouted as I took off running. I shifted into a wolf and kept running; I knew they were close behind, as I could smell them. I could also smell those vampires I met earlier who were sitting on a bench nearby. I ran up to them and started whining.

"What is it?" Robert asked, giving me a strange look.

I pawed him and tried to tell him who I was.

"Ah… sir? I think that is Liz," one man said to Robert.

"Ken, how can you tell?" Robert asked. Then he saw Tristan over by the park with another man.

"Robert, let's get her out of here to a safer place," Ken said.

Robert and Ken gave me the signal to follow them. We went inside a motorhome, and I grabbed a blanket and shifted back into human, wrapping the blanket around my cold body.

"Liz, it is you?" Robert asked with a shocked look.

"Yeah. I didn't know where else to go. Thanks," I said. I looked out the window and saw the others coming.

"Where the fuck did she go?" I heard Caleb ask as he threw the bench.

"I don't know. I can't even smell her anymore," Tristan said.

They looked right at me and I moved out of the way.

"They can't find you, my dear," Robert stated.

"How is it possible that they can't see me?" I asked.

"I put a spell on it to make the motorhome invisible to them," Robert explained.

"Cool. So you are wizard and a vampire," I said.

"Yes, I am. I'm good friends with your brother, Hunter," Robert said.

"Oh, I've heard that before. Tristan was supposed to be good friends with my father, but look what happened," I said as I looked around. The motorhome wasn't too big—it could maybe sleep six people. It was the kind you could drive, and it had a shower and washroom as well as a fridge, sink and a queen-sized bed.

"We are different. We are going to take you back to your family," Robert said as he smiled.

"How did you guys know I was here?" I asked.

"Hunter phoned me to keep an eye on you. He didn't really trust Tristan," Robert explained.

"That sounds like my brother," I said, laughing a bit.

Ken got in the driver's side and we drove to a store. Ken ran in and got some supplies, like clothing, food and beverages, and then he filled up with gas.

"Thanks for the clothing," I said, when he handed them to me. I went into the master bedroom. I thought I had closed the door all the way, so I took the blanket off and got dressed. Then I noticed the door wasn't quite closed, but I didn't say anything. I found it hard to move around in a moving vehicle. I went in the main part of the motorhome and sat down. I looked at Robert and he had this huge grin on his face.

"What is so funny?" I asked.

"I can see right through that door," Robert replied.

"No way, you bugger," I said, throwing a cup at him.

"And I liked what I saw," Robert said, smiling.

"I can tell," I said.

"Shit, I know, help me deal with it," Robert said.

"No way," I said, standing up.

"I was just kidding about you helping me," Robert replied.

"No, you weren't," I said.

"Alright, I can't lie. But Liz, seriously, I need to tell you about Tristan and Caleb. Have a seat," Robert said.

"Like what, that they are disgusting pigs and Tristan lied to me?" I said in disgust.

"Yeah. But not only that… Caleb and Tristan are planning on killing your family to get you and that diamond. That is why Tristan was more than happy to take you in," Robert explained.

"What? We have to warn them before they get to them first!" I looked around for my phone.

"That's why we are going there now," Robert said.

"I know, but shit, I left my phone at Tristan's," I said as I sat back down.

"Let's just hope they don't text your family saying you are in trouble to lure them down here," Robert said.

"Yeah, I hope not," I said. I was suddenly feeling exhausted. I yawned, got up and went to crawl into bed.

+ + +

"I feel sorry for her," Ken said to Robert as they passed the border in to Canada.

"I know. Me too. She is special and I don't know if she will ever be safe," Robert replied.

+ + +

I woke up to someone shaking me. "What? Leave me alone," I grumbled.

"Wake up, sleeping beauty. We're in Regina. Would you like something to eat?" Robert asked.

"Sure," I said. I got out of bed, got dressed and brushed my hair.

We pulled into a restaurant and we all sat down. The waitress came up to us to take our drink orders.

"You know what I realized? Last night was a full moon and I didn't change," I said, really confused.

"It's because you learning how to control it," Robert replied.

"That's cool," I said.

The waitress came by with our drinks and she got out a piece of paper and a pen. "What can I get for you today?" she asked.

"I will get the steak special, medium-rare, with baked potatoes," Robert said.

"I will get the original burger with fries. Gravy on the side," Ken said.

"I'll have an all-meat omelet with brown toast," I said. After she left, I said, "I am really worried that they got to the family first." I sipped on my coffee.

"I know, but we will be there soon," Robert stated.

The waitress came by with our food. "Enjoy," she said.

We ate our food, paid and hit the road once again. We needed to get there as fast as we could.

+ + +

"I wonder how Liz is doing. I can't get ahold of her," Blair said.

"I have a feeling that something went wrong," Kelvin stated.

There was a knock at the door, and Kelvin got up from the couch. He opened the door and he couldn't believe his eyes when he saw Caleb.

"Hello, Kelvin. Tristan and I have decided to come wait for Liz, as we know she will be here very soon," Caleb said. He laughed and shoved Kelvin aside.

"What did you do with her?" Blair asked as he glared at Tristan.

"Nothing yet," Tristan replied.

"How could you betray me, Tristan?" Blair hissed.

"Simple, actually. When you handed your precious daughter over to me it was so hard to resist that sweet fine ass, but I ended up having my way with her and she trusted me," Tristan explained as he started tying everyone up with silver-laced ropes.

"You are disgusting. What did she do to deserve this?" Jane whined.

"Oh, honey, she did nothing. Caleb went over to Jane and kissed her cheek. "By the way, don't try any of your magic because it won't work. We had a witch cast a spell amongst us so nothing can affect us." Caleb grinned.

+ + +

We finally made it home, but something seemed really wrong. I had a horrible feeling. Ken parked the motorhome across the street. When I opened the door to my house I saw all my family tied up; they looked at me, their eyes filled with fear. I knew right there and then something bad was happening. I turned around and Robert and Ken dropped to the floor, hit over the head with a steel pipe. Caleb picked them up and tied them to another chair. He looked at me and smiled. "Welcome home, honey," he said as he went behind me.

"Why can't you leave me alone?" I asked. I started to shake, I was so angry.

"What fun would that be, honey? And besides, at the end you will be coming with us," Caleb said, laughing.

"That's wishful thinking, don't you agree?" I asked as I stared at him and Tristan.

"Oh no, not at all. We planned this all out," Tristan butted in.

"You guys are disgusting," I snapped. I ran upstairs. I wanted to check up on Celina, but she was nowhere to be found.

"Liz, I wouldn't do anything stupid or someone will get hurt!" Caleb shouted.

I rolled my eyes and went back downstairs. I didn't know how I was going to get out of this one. I heard screams in the living room, and I ran to see what they were up to now.

"Honey, you're just in time to see your boyfriend get tortured," Caleb said as he whipped Kelvin with a spiked belt. Kelvin screamed in pain.

"Stop, please, I will come with you. Just please don't hurt my family," I begged as I started to cry.

"That's more like it, dear," Caleb replied. He put the whip down and came towards me.

I knew I had to go with them— what other choice did I have? It was either that or watch them torture my family. I could think of a plan to escape later, but for now I just wanted my family to be safe. I took a deep breath and followed them outside. I just kept quiet the whole ride back to Caleb's. I was so disgusted with having to be with them, and I couldn't believe I ever thought Tristan was cute. We pulled into Caleb's place and got out of the vehicle. They made sure I followed them, and they were watching me like a hawk.

"So what did you want to do tonight?" Caleb asked me.

"Not you guys," I said as I stomped past them and headed upstairs.

"I think she is pissed," Tristan said.

"She'll get over it," Caleb replied.

I lay down on the bed and stared at the canopy, just trying to think of a way out— these monsters were never going to give up. They were going to use me so they could get at that diamond, I just knew it. I had no idea what was going to happen to my family, to Celina— once they found out she was a hybrid they were going to kidnap her too.

Chapter 6

THE STAY

I was still staring at the canopy thinking when I heard footsteps outside the bedroom door. The doorknob turned and Tristan walked in. I looked at him, rolled my eyes and didn't say one word.

"Oh, come on, baby. Are you still mad?" Tristan asked as he came towards me.

"Yes! I am extremely pissed off and embarrassed," I growled as I sat up.

"You will get over it. At any rate, come downstairs to eat," Tristan demanded as he stood there waiting for me to budge.

"For your information, I won't get over it…you want to know why? I will tell you why. Because you used me, then you lied to my dad and then you had the nerve to come to my house, torture my family then leave me no choice but to come with you two disgusting monsters." I glared at him.

"That was told nicely, but anyways, I'm sorry you feel that way," Tristan said as he pulled me up by my arm and tossed me out the door.

I stomped downstairs, went into the kitchen, pulled a chair out and just sat there.

"So nice of you to join me, sweetie," Caleb stated as he came over and kissed my lips.

"Like I was left with any other choices," I said, moving away.

"Oh, don't be like that. Besides, I will never lose you again," Caleb said, grinning.

"Joy. I am thrilled," I said sarcastically as I crossed my legs.

"Look, honey, with this attitude of course you're not going to be happy. But if you changed your attitude to being happier…" Caleb said. "Anyways, I am sure you will accept your new future as my wife in a couple days, but supper is ready now so help yourself, dear," He dished himself a plate.

"I already want a divorce," I announced as I stood up and grabbed a plate. Nothing here looked appealing, but I knew I had to eat. I sighed as I dished out some food for myself.

"Oh, honey, don't be like that. I will treat you really good," Caleb replied as he kissed my neck.

+ + +

"Guys, are you ok?" Steven asked. Everyone was struggling to get free.

"Papa," Celina said as she came over to Kelvin and tugged on his rope.

"Celina, you are alive! Can you go over into the kitchen and grab Daddy a sharp object?" Kelvin asked, hoping she would understand.

Celina went into the kitchen and a few minutes later she came out with a pin. She handed it to Kelvin.

"Thank you, sweetheart," Kelvin said as he moved the pin to cut the rope and set him free. He stood up and went to cut everyone else free.

"Ok, now we need to find a way to get Liz back," Blair stated.

"Mama," Celina said as she tugged on Kelvin's arm.

"Mama is out for a bit, but she will be back," Kelvin replied as he knelt down and kissed her forehead.

"We have no idea where they took her," Hunter said, looking outside.

+ + +

I was sitting at the kitchen table trying to eat my food when there was loud knock at the door. I had a strange feeling, so I snuck out of the kitchen and headed towards upstairs.

"Who could that be?" Tristan asked as he put his drink down and got up from the kitchen table. He almost made it to the door when the door smashed open.

"Where is the girl?" the man asked as he threw Tristan into the kitchen.

"What the fuck!" Caleb shouted as he stood up and ran into the living room. "What are you fucks doing in my house?" he hissed as his eyes went red.

"Save your energy. We want the girl now," the man insisted as he stared at Caleb.

"What girl?" Caleb asked.

"Don't play dumb with us, you stupid excuse for a hybrid, we can smell her." The man shoved Caleb aside and stomped into the kitchen.

I could hear the noises, so I didn't waste any more time. I crawled out the window, and I was on top of the roof. The wind was unbelievable— it was blowing my hair around, and I could barely see. I looked around, trying to figure out the best place to jump down without them noticing me. I crawled over to the back of the house and looked down. The coast was clear. I jumped and ran through the back yard, then jumped over the fences and kept running.

+ + +

"She was here— she is so good at escaping!" Caleb yelled as he threw his kitchen chair across the kitchen. It broke into a few pieces.

"Well, you are going to help us find her," the man demanded. He went over to Caleb and lifted him up by his neck.

"Ok, I don't know who you think you are, but no one bosses me around. I am going after her for my own pleasure," Caleb answered as he kicked the air. The man let go of him, and Caleb dropped to the floor and gasped for breath.

"I don't care why you are looking for her as long as you get her," the man replied, grinning.

+ + +

I ran. I looked back to see if anyone was following me, and when I looked in front of me I ran into someone.

"Hey there. Are you alright?" a man asked me as he held on to me.

"No, I need to go!" I shouted as I shoved him aside and kept running. I didn't even have time to take a look at him, I just kept running.

+ + +

"Evan, your sweet hybrid just ran past me. She escaped out the back," the man warned Evan.

"Why didn't you grab her?" Evan asked Will.

"She moves too fast. I didn't realize that was her until now. I have never seen her... man, she is smoking," Will said.

"Yeah, she is. But she is smart. Run after her now, and we will get caught up," Evan demanded as they ran out the back door and jumped over the fences.

+ + +

I tried to cast a spell to hide my senses. I didn't have time to check if it worked. I had to keep on the lookout. I climbed up a tree in someone's back yard, as I needed to take a breather. I figured I would be safer up there than down there. I noticed a man below with a cell phone in his hand— it looked like that guy I ran into earlier. Shortly there was about four other men with him, and I knew right away they were those man-made hybrids and, of course, Tristan and Caleb. I just sat there trying not to move. My heart pumped faster as they looked around. I stood up, and I was going to climb higher when I slipped and some bark fell off and landed on one of the guys. *"Shit,"* I thought as I leaned against the tree trying to blend in.

"I think our little hybrid is up there," Evan said, pointing. He jumped up the tree, and I saw him coming. I looked around. There was a roof close by, so I jumped onto it and made a run for it once again. The men were not far behind me. I could hear them shouting at me… like that was going to make me stop for them.

"Liz, give it up!" Evan shouted.

I knew I was close to home because I could smell my family. I tried communicating with my brother through my mind.

+ + +

"Hey, you guys. Liz is talking to me," Hunter said as he closed his eyes.

"What is she saying?" Rob asked.

"Just wait," Hunter replied.

"Hunter, if you can hear me, I am very close to home and I have five men after me… can you cast a spell to shield the house?" I asked as I kept running.

"Yes, Liz, I can hear you. I will get Mother to help," Hunter replied. He opened his eyes and looked at Jane.

"Yes, Hunter. I heard everything. Here, take my hand and repeat after me," Jane said. She took Hunter's hand and they started chanting a spell.

+ + +

I could still hear them behind me. I could see my house up ahead, and I ran faster. I jumped off the roofs onto the ground and went flying inside. "Now!" I yelled as I locked the doors. I looked out the window and they came flying at the house, but as soon as they came near it they went flying backwards.

"Fuck! What the… we can't get in!" Tristan said.

"She got her family to cast a spell around the house. I can fix that, though. I will go find a witch," Caleb said, laughing as he left the yard.

"Liz, are you alright?" Hunter asked as he hugged me.

"Yeah, for now. What about you guys?" I asked. I looked around to make sure everyone was accounted for.

"Yeah, we are fine," Hunter replied.

"Look, we don't have much time. We need to figure out a plan," I said.

"I know, but they are very strong," Blair noted.

"I know. But so am I, and so are you guys," I pointed out.

"I was looking forward to getting a closer look at our hybrid," Will said, disappointed.

"You will have your chance. Besides, Will, you really need to get laid," Mickey said as he patted Will on his back.

"I know. That's why I want Liz," Will replied, licking his lips.

I stepped outside to see what they were doing. They were just sitting there patiently.

"There she is," Will pointed out as he elbowed Mickey.

"I know, we see her. Are you obsessed with her?" Mickey asked, giving Will a strange look.

"Kind of. She is fascinating," Will replied.

"Boys, why don't you give up," I said, smiling as I leaned against the house.

"No way, honey," Will said, staring at me.

"I know what you want with me," I said in disgust as I went back inside.

"They are not going to leave, honey," Kelvin pointed out.

"I know, but it was worth a try," I replied as I took a deep breath in. I looked out the window and I saw Caleb storming back into my yard. He had a girl with him.

+ + +

"Now, honey, do your magic. Take their shield off the house," Caleb demanded as he looked at his watch.

"I am not an experienced witch," the young girl responded.

"I don't care. Just do it," Caleb snapped.

+ + +

"Guys, tell me if I am wrong, but I think they are using a witch to counteract the shield," I said as I watched through the window.

"You are probably right," Steven answered as he came and looked out the window with me.

The girl she was pretty young, and was dark-skinned, very petite and had black long hair. She was closing her eyes and chanting some words. It wasn't long before I could feel the forcefield getting weaker and weaker.

"Mother, Hunter, and Robert! I'm sure as two witches and two wizards we can think of something!" I shouted.

"Come, honey, get in this circle. We will summon a demon to get rid of them for now," my mother said. I sat down and held her and Hunter's hands. We all started chanting, and we had candles burning all around us. Soon it got very windy, and the lights shuddered off and on.

"Sir, they are casting another spell. I am not sure what for, but I can feel the magic," the young witch said as she looked at Caleb.

"Fuck. I will go inside then and deal with this," Caleb said, storming away. He entered the house but a wave of negative energy hit him and he fell to the floor in pain. We didn't pay attention; we kept chanting, and the demon got stronger and stronger. We could hear Caleb screaming, and I opened my eyes just in time to see a dark shadow with red eyes come flying towards him. He got up and ran out of the house.

"What is going on, Caleb?" Tristan asked as he headed towards the house.

"I wouldn't go in there. They are chanting a spell to release some kind of demon, and it is very strong," Caleb replied as he wiped the sweat off his forehead.

"Well, isn't this lovely. How are we going to get the girl?" Mickey snapped.

"We will think of something," Evan said. "She can't escape that easily." He grinned.

+ + +

We let go of each other's hands, and as we opened our eyes everything stopped. I slowly got up to look outside and see if they had given up, for now at least. I couldn't see anyone, but I didn't trust them. "I have a funny feeling about this. I can't see them anywhere, but I think they are probably up to no good," I said.

"I know they are up to no good. They would never give up that easily," Mark stated.

"You two better think of a way to get our girl back," Evan snapped.

"We are trying," Caleb snapped back.

"What about our witch?" Will asked as he looked at her.

"I'm sorry, guys, but I can't compete with them. There are four against one," the young witch explained.

"Look, sweetie, what is your name?" Evan asked, holding his hands together and sighing.

"Lisa," she answered, looking scared.

"Ok, Lisa, honey, you are going to try your best," Evan said. He shoved her towards the house.

"I don't even know what they are doing... oh wait, I can see their witch. She's coming towards the house," I noted. I stepped outside to see if I could see the guys.

"Well, our witch didn't have to do anything to lure our hybrid out... she decided to be a good little girl and come out herself," Evan said. He came to grab me and he grabbed my wrist but I looked at him and he went flying backwards.

"Don't piss me off!" I shouted, glaring at him. "I have had it with you guys chasing after me. Just leave me alone," I snapped as I watched Evan get back up.

"That was entertaining, honey, but I am sorry. We can't leave you be," Evan said. He lunged at me, turning into a hybrid, and I jumped over him, landing behind him. I used my witch powers to make him freeze in that one spot. I tried to catch my breath, but it was becoming so unbearable I felt like I was going to pass out. How was I ever going to get rid of them once and for all?

Chapter 7

THE IMAGINABLE

Here I was outside with five maniacs, three of them man-made hybrids, one an obsessive hybrid and the other one a creepy old vampire who, I might add, I slept with. I looked back at Evan. He was still frozen. I heard the other guys shift, and I turned and suddenly and there stood three more hybrids. *"Liz, what did you get yourself into?"* I thought as I backed up. The door flew open and out came Hunter and Kelvin.

"Guys, what are you doing?" I asked as I stepped further away from the others.

"We are here to help. You're not the only hybrid," Hunter pointed out as he shifted.

"I have never shifted, but I guess I will try," Kelvin said as he closed his eyes. I watched him scream as his bones cracked and hair covered his whole body and his back legs bent inwards… actually, it was kind of gross watching it from another hybrid's view.

"I guess it's my turn," I said to myself as I shifted. All three of us stood there growling at the other hybrids.

"You guys are shit out of luck… there are three against four," Tristan said as he laughed.

Then in the corner of my eye I saw my dad come flying out the door. He lunged at Tristan. "You asshole! You lied to me, and you hurt my daughter!" He threw Tristan against a tree, but Tristan just laughed. He got up and lunged back at Blair. I stood there growling at the other hybrids. When Caleb stood up and bit my neck I howled in pain, turned around and gashed Caleb across the face. We started fighting as the other three ran towards Hunter and Kelvin, and soon there was a huge fight.

"Let me tell you, your daughter is one of a hell a lay," Tristan said as he knocked Blair down to the ground and held a stake up to his heart. Blair grabbed a rock and smashed it over Tristan's head. He fell to the ground holding his head, and Blair slowly got up, picked Tristan up and tossed him into the house.

Caleb and I were making this fight personal. We were only fighting amongst ourselves, and it was getting gruesome. Between all of us hybrids fighting there was blood splattering everywhere. I'm sure people could hear us yelp all the way across town… it was a wonder why police were not showing up to tranquilize us. That might be the best thing yet. I was about to bite Caleb once again when he suddenly stood in complete silence and fell to the ground. So did the others; they all shifted back into their human forms. I shifted back too. Standing there naked and freezing to death surrounded by collapsed hybrids, even Hunter and Kelvin were affected, but not me… why?" I asked myself.

I looked across the road and that young witch smiled at me and took off… could it be that she did this?" I went inside to grab something to cover up with. Tristan and my father were still lashing it out on each other. I walked right in the middle and yelled, "Stop, you two, right now!" They both froze and stared at me. They were catching their breath. "Ok, now that I have your attention, all the other hybrids collapsed except me. Don't ask me why, I have no idea," I said as I went back outside to check up on them. They all slowly got up, coughing and wiping the dirt off their wounded bodies.

"So, boys, do you want to keep fighting or can we call it a night? I personally prefer the second option because I am lazy and tired," I explained.

"Liz, wait," Evan said.

"What?" I asked as I turned around.

"Can we come inside and warm up please? We will be good," Evan asked, shivering.

"Ha! Why in the world would I trust you? I mean, come on, you guys have been chasing me and fighting me for a long time now and you want to make a truce with me and my family? I'm sorry, but I don't think so. I don't know who you think I am, but I am not stupid or naive," I headed back inside.

Evan came running up to me and grabbed my arm. "Please. I know. I don't blame you… just let me explain why we have been after you," he pleaded.

I looked at him and the other boys. I crossed my arms. "Fine, but hurry before I change my mind," I said as I stormed inside.

The boys followed behind me. I went upstairs to my bedroom to get a change of clothing. I was rummaging through my drawers when I felt someone behind me. "Look, I am not in the mood. I'm going to get changed," I snapped. I turned around.

"I'm sorry. I was just going to ask where the washroom was," Will asked.

"Sorry. It's down the hallway to your right," I said as I pointed it out to him. He just stood there staring at me.

"Do I need to hold your hand?" I hissed.

"No. I am waiting for you to get changed. I want to watch," Will replied, smiling.

"Nice try," I said as I tossed him out of my room and shut the door behind him.

I got dressed and went downstairs. I didn't want to leave those freaks with my family for too long.

"What's up?" I asked as I plopped down on the couch next to Kelvin.

"Not a whole lot," Kelvin replied.

"So, Evan, are you going to explain to me what is going on?" I asked, facing him.

"Yes. There are people higher up than us whose mission is to kidnap you so we can continue making more hybrids," Evan explained.

"Ok, and what about the part where you guys mate with me?" I asked, confused.

"Well, that was our second plan if the first plan didn't work," Evan replied.

"What was the first plan, if I might ask?" I asked.

"To take your blood then inject it into our spines. It took us a long time to figure it out," Evan said.

"So now what… are you hybrids forever?" I asked.

"No. We have to keep injecting a pure hybrid's blood into us," Evan explained.

"Ok, so now I know why you are after me. Just for the record, I am not too peachy living my life donating my blood," I said as I got up and headed toward the kitchen.

"Ok, time's up. I don't like these fake hybrids here, or Caleb or Tristan, for that matter," Tyler said, standing up.

"What are you going to do about it, wolf boy?" Tristan said as he laughed in Tyler's face.

Tyler shoved Tristan across the floor. Tristan stood up and flew at Tyler, knocking him into the wall.

"Enough!" I shouted, standing between them. "Tyler, I decide when they leave. Besides, I need to know all the details."

"Tyler, I think Liz is getting sick of all the fighting. In fact, we all are," Steven blurted out.

"These assholes won't leave Liz alone!" Tyler shouted as he opened the door. He was about to step outside when he was shocked and sent flying backwards.

"What the hell happened?" I asked as I ran towards Tyler. I shook him but he was out cold.

"Our witch put a spell on this house so no one can go anywhere," Caleb laughed. He stood up and looked down at Tyler. "What a pathetic excuse for a werewolf," He growled as he kicked him.

"Stop. I can't handle any more fighting!" I shouted. I shoved Caleb in to the wall. "Why did you have her cast a spell on my house? And you do realize there are two witches and two wizards here!" I pinned Caleb down.

"Oh, my dearest Liz, you just don't fucking get it, do you?" Caleb hissed as he touched my face.

"Get what? And don't touch me," I snarled. I was just about to bite him when I could smell something burning.

"Caleb, grab the girl. This is our queue," Evan said. They grabbed me and bolted out the door.

Before I could react, I was hit over the head with a large chunk of wood. "What a girl," Caleb said as he picked me up.

I woke up hours later, groggy, with no idea where I was. I managed to open my eyes a bit and look around. I was strapped to a wooden chair, and my wrists were bound by silver rope. The rope burned my wrists, and I started screaming in pain. I heard a door open and footsteps come closer to me.

"Liz, how nice, you're awake," the man's voice said as he knelt down beside me and licked my face.

"Caleb, what did you do?" I asked as I tried moving my wrists up and down.

"Well, first we had some of our best witches remove your family's magic, then our dearest friend Mickey was outside the whole time and he set your house on fire with your family in it," Caleb said, laughing.

"No, no, no, you asshole, you're going to pay!" I said. I tried to shift, but I was way too weak.

"No, we are not, baby," Caleb said as he chuckled and left the room.

The room was cold and dark, and it smelled like dirt and mold. *What was going to happen to my family?* I asked myself. I sat there not knowing what to do anymore. I just wanted to give up... this was the end, this was it. I continued to scope the room. I could feel my eyes getting heavy. I must have fallen asleep, because I woke up to water being poured all over me and a pail dropping to the concrete flooring. The sound echoed throughout the room. I shot straight up and screamed.

"Baby, you like getting wet, don't you?" Tristan said. He grabbed my face and made me look at him.

"You're disgusting. I will find a way out. I always do," I said as I squirmed around in my chair.

"Think what you want," Tristan said as he backhanded me.

I spit some blood out of my mouth and growled at him. My wrists were raw from the rope digging into them, and they became painless. I could hear them fiddling around with something. I tried to make it out, but I couldn't. Caleb came towards me and stuck a needle in my vein; blood poured down a clear tube into a glass vial, and eventually caused me to pass out.

"I don't think she has eaten anything since we brought her here," Tristan said as he gathered up the vials and put them in a blue carrying case marked *bio-hazard*.

"You're probably right. I will go get our little hybrid something," Caleb said as he took the needle out of my arm and put it away in a plastic container.

"Liz, wake up, dear," Tristan said as he grabbed my face and slapped me a few times.

"What do you want now?" I growled in his face.

"Eat," Tristan demanded as he opened my mouth and poured blood down my throat.

I didn't argue this one. I drank it fast; I was so hungry. I still wasn't strong enough, but they knew what they were doing. They didn't want me strong, but they wanted to keep me alive. I was waiting until they released me from this chair then maybe I could think of a way to escape and see if my family made it out safe. I heard footsteps outside the door, so I acted like I was dead. I shut down my breathing just enough to give a very weak pulse. They couldn't lose me, so they would have no choice but to untie me. The door flew open and Mickey walked in.

"Wake up, sleeping beauty, time to get to work," Mickey demanded as he shook me. "Liz, wake up. Liz. Guys, something is wrong!" Mickey shouted at Caleb and Tristan.

They bolted towards me. "Check her pulse," Tristan said as he looked at Mickey.

Mickey put his fingers on my neck, and he looked up at them. "It is very faint. We must get her to the doctor. We can't lose her." Mickey untied me, picked me up and carried me to a room. he lay me down on a bed and waited.

I could sense someone else come in, and it was human for sure.

"Hello, doctor, we need you to help our little hybrid," Mickey said.

What? Why would they tell the doctor what I was? Of course, the doctor was working for them. Why else would the doctor be working at their base.

"Of course, Mickey, what seems to the problem?" the doctor asked with his English accent.

"Her pulse is very faint," Mickey said.

I could smell the doctor coming towards me. He knelt down beside me and I could hear his breathing. This was my chance. I opened my eyes and bit the doctor's neck. He screamed in pain as he struggled to break free. I fed until the doctor became lifeless, and then dropped him to the floor. I wiped the blood from my mouth, looked over at the boys and smiled. Their mouths dropped.

"You fooled us once again, little girl," Mickey said as he walked towards me.

I stared at him intently. He dropped to the floor in pain, covering his ears. I looked at the other boys and they too dropped to the floor in pain. I got up and walked right past them. On the way out, there were about five men dressed in army uniforms with guns shooting at me. I had a barrier that surrounded me. I looked at them they dropped like flies and bled from their eyes, nose and ears. As soon as I left the building I darted it, jumping over the fence and smelling my way back home. I was so scared that I was going to find my family dead. What would I do? Where would I go?

Chapter 8

STAY STRONG

I finally made it back home only to find my house all burnt. It was barely standing. I stood there crying; there was no sign of my family. I couldn't even smell them. I had no idea what to do. I couldn't stick around, or those monsters would be after me. I walked over to Daniel's. He was the only one who knew about me that I could trust.

I took my time walking there. *What was the point anymore?* I asked myself as I walked along the riverbank. I sat on the bench and stared at the river as it flowed by. I could tell by the dark clouds it was going to rain, so I stood up and continued to walk. About fifteen minutes later I approached Daniel's house. His house was white and there was a little wooden deck you walked up to get to the front door. He had a few shrubs that surrounded the front of the house. I knocked on his door and waited. I could hear footsteps, and the door swung open.

"Liz, wow, you don't look so good. Come in," Daniel said as he hugged me and directed me inside his house.

His house was small the living room had one tan loveseat, and a flat screen TV that hung on the wall. He had a collection of monster figures on a shelf in the living room. His kitchen had laminate flooring and he had a small brown pedestal table. He had an old green stove to go along with his fridge.

"Thanks, Daniel. I didn't know where else to go," I replied.

"It's ok. Tell me what happened. Go wait for me in the living room. Would you like anything to drink?" Daniel asked.

"No, I'm fine," I said as I walked in to the living room and sat on the couch.

Daniel sat next to me and placed his hand on my knee. He looked so concerned.

"Caleb is a hybrid who is after me along with his accomplice, Tristan, who is a vampire. Tristan was supposed to my dad's friend and I stayed with him over in the States… needless to say, he betrayed him. Then these man-made hybrids are after me too. So all these monsters are after me to create more hybrids—well, Caleb is after me because he wants to marry me, but let's not get in to that. So they burned my house down, kidnapped me and now I am sure my family is dead. I don't know what to do," I said, ranting on. I could barely breathe.

"Just take a deep breath. We will figure this out," Daniel said as he hugged me.

"I know. I am getting so sick of this bullshit," I replied as I looked away.

"Hey. You're strong. You can get through this," Daniel replied, touching my face.

"You're right. Do you mind if I stay here for a few days until I can figure out something?" I asked, smiling at him.

"Yes, of course. I have a spare room upstairs," Daniel said.

"Thanks. How can I repay you?" I asked.

"There is one thing. I want to be a hybrid, please," Daniel said, begging.

"No. It is too dangerous," I replied. I could see the frustration on his face.

"I know the consequences and I am willing to deal with them. I'm so fascinated with your kind," Daniel responded as he grabbed my wrist.

"Just let me think about it," I said as I removed my hand. "If you will excuse me, I am going for walk. I will be back," I said. I got up, got my shoes on and headed out the front door. It was raining hard. I headed down the back alley and stared at the ground as I walked. I heard screams just a few blocks up ahead and ran towards them. I saw two average-sized men wearing white hoodies and blue jeans. They had their hoods up and they had a young girl pinned up against a brown broken-down fence. She was crying. Black streams of mascara ran down her face, and her brown hair covered her eyes. She was wearing a pink sweater and black jeans. One of the men had a knife, and he was waving it in her face.

"Give us his number, bitch!" one of the men screamed at her.

She cried even harder and turned her face away. She saw me standing there. The one guy grabbed her face and when she struggled to look back, I was gone.

"Talk, bitch, or…"

"Or what?" I asked as I snapped the guy's neck. He fell to the ground. The other guys looked at me and ran. I stared at the girl. She just stood there in shock.

"Forget what you saw here," I said as I used some witch magic to make her forget what had just happened. She nodded and walked the opposite direction.

I smelled the air around me. I needed to find that other guy before he found her again. I found him behind a broken-down house with a group of friends. I overheard one guy talking to his friends about the strange occurrence that just happened. I walked towards them, trying to see if he recognized me.

"Hey, man, do you have a smoke?" I asked.

"No, sorry, cutie," the guy from the alley responded as he stared at me. "You're the girl that killed my friend… how did you do that?" he asked as he stepped away from me.

"What did you want with that girl anyways?" I asked, moving closer. His friends pulled out a pocket knife, ready to protect him.

"I'm not telling you," he replied, shoving me.

I turned around and lifted my hand. The other guys stood still; they couldn't move. "Now you're going to tell me," I snapped as I walked towards him. "If you touch me again, I will rip you apart."

"What are you?" he asked as he started to run.

I ran right in front of him, pushed him to the ground and bit into his neck. I tore his chest up and tore right into him. He screamed for a bit and kicked his legs, but a few seconds later he became still. I stood up and wiped the blood off my face. I smiled and continued walking. I walked back to Daniel's and saw two men standing at the front door. Caleb and Tristan. I turned to walk in the other direction, but Mickey spotted me.

"There she is!" Mickey shouted as he bolted after me.

I ran into Daniel in the yard.

"Daniel, you need to hide me," I said, looking up at him.

"No, I'm sorry, but I am handing you over," Daniel said as he flagged Mickey down.

"No! What? why?" I asked, starting to shake.

"They promised me they would turn me in return for you," Daniel replied as he chuckled.

"Thank you, Daniel," Mickey said as he grabbed me and kissed my lips.

"Yuck, you're disgusting," I said, pushing him away.

"So do I get to turn now?" Daniel asked.

"I'm sorry, Daniel, my poor boy," Mickey said as he flagged Evan.

Evan came behind Daniel and bit his neck. Daniel screamed and fell to the ground. Blood poured down his shirt and all around his body.

"No!" I screamed as I struggled to be free.

"Sucks, doesn't?" Mickey said. He pushed me into a black truck that had pulled up.

We were riding down a dirt road when I bit the driver. He screamed and the truck went rolling. I slowly opened my eyes and there was glass everywhere. The other guys looked like they were knocked out, and blood dribbled down their face. I ripped the seat belt off, turned around and kicked the door, and it went flying. I crawled out and limped away. I needed to get as far away from Prince

Albert as I could. I didn't have money or a vehicle. I knew what I had to do to survive. I walked along the highway that went to Saskatoon, sticking out my thumb. I needed to hitchhike. Vehicles kept driving by, not even acknowledging me.

Finally, a white sporty car pulled over. The passenger window rolled down. I peeked in and there was a man sitting there with short curly brown hair with so much gel in it that it looked almost like plastic. His sunglasses were black and purple and covered half his face. He pulled his sunglasses down, showing his brown eyes, and he smiled.

"Get in, gorgeous," he said as he unlocked his door.

I looked around and got in. I closed the door and put my seat belt on. I noticed that he kept playing with his tongue ring. It was kind of irritating me.

"My name is Doug," he said as he turned the AC on.

"My name is Liz," I replied.

"Where are you going?" Doug asked.

"I guess Saskatoon," I replied.

"Ok. By the way, why is a beautiful young girl like you hitchhiking anyways?" Doug asked, shooting me a strange look.

"Problems in my life," I replied, looking away.

I knew what I had to do. I had to bite him and steal his money and his car. I really had no choice. The whole drive was awkward. We finally arrived in Saskatoon and he took me to his hotel.

"Doug, what are we doing?" I asked.

"I'm taking you to my room. You owe me," Doug said, smiling.

At first I was thinking no, but then I saw I could use this to my advantage. "Ok, fair enough," I said. I got out of the passenger side and followed him to the room.

We got into his room and I pushed him down on the bed. I got on top of him and started kissing his lips. His hands wandered my body and I moaned. I took his pants off and he took my shirt off, revealing my pink lacy bra. I stood up and took my black yoga pants off and my pink lacy panties slid down my legs. His mouth dropped. He pulled me closer into him and kissed me. I pushed back down and pulled his grey boxers down. I slid down, inserting him into me, and we both moaned. I kissed his neck, and his hands were on my hips. He started pushing harder and moaning and he released inside me. He smiled at me, I smiled back, and then my eyes turned purple.

"What the hell?" Doug said as he tried pushing me off.

"Sorry, sweetheart, thanks for your car and for the good time," I replied. As I bit his neck, I covered his mouth. After he stopped moving I got off and covered his dead body with the white sheet. I got dressed, fixed my hair up, found his wallet and keys and made my way out. I walked out of the hotel room like nothing happened. I was actually starting to enjoy living my life like this. No one could stop me; I was so strong. I hopped in the white car and took off, heading towards the Regina highway. When I got into the city I pulled into a gas station. I got out and put the gas nozzle in the tank and started pumping. I was minding my own business when I heard someone talking behind me.

"Excuse me, miss, do you have a lighter?" a soft voice asked.

"No, sorry, I don't smoke," I replied. I turned around and there stood a petite young girl. Her blue eyes sparkled in the sun, and her brown curly hair bounced on her shoulders.

She smiled at me and softly replied back, "That's ok."

I noticed she was wearing a wolf necklace. I was very intrigued by this girl… there was something about her.

"My name is Vanessa," she said, holding out her hand.

"I'm Liz," I replied as I shook her hand.

"Say, did you want to grab some coffee just over there at that small café?" Vanessa asked, still holding her unlit cigarette.

"Sure, just let me finish up and we can go over there together," I replied as I shot her a little smile.

I finished filling the tank and headed inside to pay. I watched Vanessa from the window. She just stood there looking around, the wind blowing her perfectly curled hair. She was such a cute little girl. I finished paying and headed towards the car.

"Are you ready?" I asked as I got in the driver's side. I unlocked the car so she could get in.

"Yeah," Vanessa replied as she got in.

Just about a block away from the gas station there was a small café, so I pulled in. I parked the car and we stepped out. As soon as we walked in, everyone stopped and turned around to stare at us. It was very nerve-wracking. We tried to ignore them and continued to walk towards the front counter. We both ordered small skinny lattes and ventured to find a seat.

"So, Liz, where are you from?" Vanessa asked as she blew on her hot drink.

"I'm from Prince Albert, and you?" I asked as I did the same thing.

"I am from here, born and raised. What brings you here?" Vanessa asked.

"I'm on a road trip. I just needed to get away," I replied.

Vanessa kind of looked at me funny, as though for some reason she didn't believe me. "So where are you heading?" she asked as she took a little sip from her latte.

"I'm staying the night here and then my next stop will probably be Winnipeg," I replied.

"Where is your family?" Vanessa asked, completely ignoring the other question she just asked me.

"They died in a house fire. I would rather not talk about it," I said.

"I am sorry. My family is gone to," Vanessa replied.

I was hoping we would be going soon. This place stunk like sweat and coffee. It was gross. It was getting very loud in there, but I didn't want to make it obvious I wanted to go.

"Can I come with you to the hotel?" Vanessa asked.

"I guess," I replied.

We finally finished our drinks and headed outside. We got back into the car and sped off to the nearest hotel. "Actually, Liz, you can stay at my house," Vanessa piped up.

"Ok, that sounds good," I said, smiling.

She told me the directions to her house and we finally arrived. Her small house was white with chipped paint. There was a broken-down brown fence that surrounded it. I pulled into a small gravel driveway that was covered in grass and weeds. We got out of the car and headed for the front door, and she pulled her keys out and unlocked the door. Her door made a squealing noise as she opened it. Her kitchen was small, with olive-green appliances, she had a small wooden round table with two wooden chairs tucked in. The living room had a brown carpet and an old wood stove, and she had a ripped-up orange couch and wooden rocking chair next to the stove. The floor creaked as you stepped on it. I spotted the same wolf statue I had. It was on a shelf beside the small TV.

"You have the same wolf statue as me," I said.

"Yeah, my mother gave it to me," Vanessa replied.

Could it be? I didn't think I had a sister… I needed to ask her more. I needed to find out. Could I really have a sister? If so, was she a hybrid like me? Those others could be in for a huge surprise.

Chapter 9

MY OTHER HALF

"Vanessa, do you know anything about your family?" I asked as I kept staring at the statue.

"Not really," she said as she came and stood beside me.

"This is going to be a strange request, but can we smash this statue?" I asked as I picked it up.

"No, why?" Vanessa said, taking it from me.

"Because I had the same one, and it fell off my shelf and smashed. As I was picking up the pieces, I came across a scroll written in German. So I called my friend Daniel and he translated the script for me. It said that my family came from a lycanthrope bloodline, meaning I am a werewolf. Trust me, I thought it was crazy, but sure enough, next full moon I transformed," I explained as I looked at her blue eyes.

"Are you crazy? You expect me to believe that?" Vanessa replied, glaring at me.

"I know you don't want to believe it. I didn't want to either, but it was true, and if this is true then that means you are my sister," I said.

"If you are right, then what would happen to me?" Vanessa asked.

"I would take care of you. I am a hybrid and a witch. There are strange men after me. They want to make more hybrids, and if you are a hybrid we will have to stick together because those men are going to love the fact that there are two female hybrids," I said as I took the wolf statue from her hands and dropped it onto the floor. It broke into a few pieces. Sure enough, there was a scroll lying there in the pieces of the statue. I picked it up and it was written in German—the same as mine.

"What does it say?" Vanessa asked, looking very concerned.

"I can't read it, but it is the same as mine so I'm assuming it says you are a werewolf," I explained.

"What do I do?" Vanessa said. She put her hands over her head and paced back and forth.

"I will take you with me. I am not leaving you alone," I said. I stopped her and hugged her.

"Ok, it will be ok. I just need to get packed," Vanessa said. She went upstairs and a few moments later she came back downstairs with a purple duffle bag.

"We need to stop at a store. I need to grab some clothing," I said as we headed out the front door.

We got in the car and drove off. I stopped at the nearest store and ran in. As I was in the store, I spotted a man that looked Tristan. I got scared and picked up a few things. I saw the man look at me and he smiled and started walking towards me. I ran the other way, went to the nearest till and got the hell out of there. I kept looking back. I ran to the car, opened the truck and put our purchases in there. I shut the trunk, jumped in the car and sped off in a rush. I looked at Vanessa, and she could see the fear in my eyes.

"What happened?" Vanessa asked.

"Tristan is there. I am not sure about the others," I replied.

I kept driving. I didn't want to stop anywhere— not if those idiots were in town. We finally made our way out of Regina and got on the highway to Winnipeg.

"So what is it like to be what you are?" Vanessa asked.

"It is scary. I am very powerful, but I need to feed on blood otherwise I get weak and I will die," I replied.

"Was it scary when you first turned into a werewolf?" Vanessa asked.

"Let me tell you the story. After finding that scroll, I was kidnapped by another werewolf named Tyler. We fell in love, and he helped me out. On the night of the full moon, two men came by and took us, put us in a cage and we transformed in there. It was scary. My bones cracked and my body hurt, but you get used to it. Ever since then I have been running away from bad people. Now there are these man-made hybrids using my blood to transform themselves into hybrids."

Her jaw dropped. "I'm scared," she said.

"I know. I was too, but I am here for you," I said, reassuring her.

She sighed and continued to stare out the window. I knew she was nervous by the way she was twiddling her thumbs, and she would look at me for a couple seconds and quickly turn away. "Does it hurt?" Vanessa asked as she continued to stare out the window.

"I am not going to lie, yes it does, but you become used to the pain," I answered. I turned on some AC, as it was getting way too hot.

After a long six-hour drive we finally made it to Winnipeg. I was trying to find Conrad's house. I had an idea where it was. I remembered driving down this gravel road and turning down a long driveway. I finally found his place, and Vanessa and I got out of the car. We started walking towards the front door when a mangy-looking vampire came running out after us; he was waving his broom at us and swearing and yelling. His long black beard ran down his chest, and his thin long black hair was blowing in the wind as he ran. He started hitting me with the broom and yelling at me. "Get out of here, you demon bitch! Conrad was killed because of you!" the old vampire yelled as he hit me.

I rolled my eyes and stared at him. He held his head and fell to the ground, blood pouring down from his eyes. "Look, asshole, how about you don't fuck with me and I won't fuck with you. Besides, Conrad had it coming," I said with a smirk. I kicked him in the face and he went flying backwards and screamed in pain. I looked over at Vanessa, and she looked terrified.

"Come on, let's get you inside," I said as I lead the way into Conrad's house.

It still looked the same. Nothing had changed— the smells, and even the mess.

"If Conrad is dead? Who is looking after this house?" Vanessa asked as she looked around.

"I don't have a clue. Probably that mangy vampire outside," I said, laughing.

I heard laughter behind me, and suddenly my hair was grabbed. Before I could even fight back, I was thrown to the floor. Before getting up I was kicked in the ribs. I started coughing. I grabbed my side in pain; now I was pissed off. I slowly got up and turned around. I stared into Caleb's eyes. I wanted to rip that grin off his face.

"So nice of you find us," I growled.

"Oh, honey, you are such a fighter! I am done playing your fun little games. By the way, who is this little girl?" Caleb asked as he smiled at her.

"You touch her and I will kill you," I snarled as I stepped in front of Vanessa. "In fact, I should kill you, Mickey, and Tristan for killing my family, you fuckers."

"You're a funny girl. You can't kill me," Caleb snapped back as he looked over to his right and Tristan and Mickey stepped into the room. "Now you are going to tell me who this fine young lady is," Caleb said as he grabbed my face and force-kissed me.

I shoved him and wiped my lips. "You're disgusting," I replied as I held onto Vanessa.

"I am scared. What is happening?" Vanessa asked as she looked at Tristan and Mickey.

"I know, I don't blame you," I replied. I didn't know how we were going to escape. I mean, I knew I was strong, but there were three of them against... well, just me. Vanessa didn't know her powers yet. I mean, she had never transformed yet. Plus, I had to protect her too.

"Hey, Caleb, we can have some fun with both these girls," Mickey said, laughing as he shuffled his way towards us. He started smelling Vanessa and she stood there in fear. "Funny, this girl smells lovely," Mickey stated as he pulled her back and smelled her more intensely.

Could he really smell that she was a werewolf? How? He was a man-made hybrid, so how could he have the senses of a real hybrid? That was impossible. I kept asking myself this over and over again, my heart racing. I didn't want this to happen to my sister.

"What do you mean, she smells lovely?" Tristan and Caleb both asked, curious.

"She smells like Liz," Mickey said, smiling.

"That is impossible. There is only one female hybrid," Caleb said as he stared into Vanessa's eyes. "Are you a werewolf?" Caleb asked as her.

"I... I don't know," Vanessa said, trembling in fear.

"Leave her alone, Caleb," I said. I shoved him and he went flying and hit the wall. I really shouldn't have done that. I just pissed him off.

He got up and started growling, and his eyes turned a red colour. He started to shift. I grabbed Vanessa and booked it out of the house. We ran into a nearby forest. I marked the trees in my blood to confuse them. I saw an old cabin just up ahead.

"Vanessa, up there. It's a cabin," I said. We went up to the door and I knocked. A few seconds later an older lady opened the door. She smiled, and her green eyes stared at us as she welcomed us in. It was almost like she was expecting us. She was wearing a purple dress, and her grey hair was done up in a bun. She had rings on all fingers, but one thing I noticed the most was a pink crystal necklace— it was beautiful.

"My name is Anne. Have a seat, girls," Anne said as she headed in the kitchen.

Her cabin was small, and she had an old stove in the living room. Her couch was red, and she had a wooden rocking chair. The house smelled like spices and smoke.

"Are you girls hungry?" Anne called.

"Yes, please," we both said.

"Ok," Anne replied as she came into the living room with bowls of stew.

We were both starving, and we didn't say a word until we were done. We set our bowls on a little wooden coffee table in front of the couch.

"Thanks, that was great," we said as we rubbed our stomachs. "By the way, I'm Liz and this is Vanessa," I said.

"There is no need to introduce yourselves. I already know who you are. I was expecting you two at some point," Anne explained.

"How"? I asked.

"I am your great-grandmother. I cast that spell on you girls not to turn until you turn twenty-four. Vanessa, dear, I know this is scary, but Liz did it and I know you can too. I know this is a lot for the both of you, but stay strong and stick together. And Liz, I know you will teach your sister the ways since she is the same as you. As for those monsters, they will stop at nothing and they will come here looking for you, so you can't stay here long. I will try and stall them as long as I can. I made you these necklaces." Anne handed us necklaces with wolves howling on pink crystals.

"Thanks. Do you know how I kill them?" I asked.

"They are very hard to kill right now. I would worry about keeping Vanessa safe. She will undergo her transformation tomorrow night," Anne said.

We heard our names being called, and we knew they were close.

"Ok, you need to leave. Go out my back door. I will stall them," Anne said. She looked at us with fear in her eyes.

"Thanks for everything, and be careful," I said as Vanessa and I left through the back door.

Back at the cabin, Anne heard a knock at the door. "Coming." She opened the door and Caleb, Mickey and Tristan stood there. "Do you know where Liz is?" Caleb asked.

"No, and even if I did I wouldn't tell you," Anne hissed as she put a spell on her cabin so they couldn't hurt her.

"You're a brave old women. I bet you are a witch," Caleb said. He tried to reach for Anne, but he went flying backwards.

"You're smart, but you're barking up the wrong tree. My granddaughters are tough. They come from the most powerful bloodline of hybrids; the first girls to be lycans, vampires and witches. They are a pureblood hybrid from the Garou bloodline, and if I were you I would back down," Anne explained as she slammed her door.

"Have it your way. We will get those girls," Caleb said as he stood there in anger.

"So it is true about that other girl," Tristan said.

"I guess so," Caleb said. "We need to shift so we can find them easier."

+ + +

"Liz, I'm getting tired, and I don't feel well," Vanessa cried.

"Ok. We will have to hide out in the forest. Maybe a cave or something," I answered.

"Are you kidding? What about wolves?" Vanessa asked.

"Vanessa, you are a werewolf and tomorrow you will be transforming," I reminded her. "Besides, those wolves are our friends. If we howl, they will come to our side. Wolves are stronger as a pack," I explained, trying to make her feel better.

"That makes sense," Vanessa said, yawning.

It was getting late out and we found a small cave. We crawled inside. "Liz, what do those men want?" Vanessa asked.

"They want to mate with us and make hybrid babies," I answered. "It isn't pretty. I have been running for a long time now." I yawned too.

We had only been asleep awhile when we woke up to howling. I went out of the cave to see if I could see the wolves. I looked over in the trees and saw red eyes coming closer. "Shit, Vanessa, they found us, but they are in their wolf form."

"What are we going to do?" Vanessa asked as she came out and stood beside me.

"I don't know. I mean, I can shift but I know you can't yet. Besides, I am too weak. I don't even think I can use magic." I felt sick. I could hear them coming closer, and their growls punctured my ears. How was I going to get out of this one? I was too weak to do anything. I thought I was going to collapse, but I needed to protect my sister. It was too much, though. I could feel myself getting weaker. I fell to the ground and I was out.

I woke up tied to a bed. I couldn't even move. The room was dark and very quiet. I knew exactly who kidnapped me. I was so weak, and I needed to feed. I could hear faint footsteps… they got louder and then the squeal from the door hurt my ears.

"Well, is my little wolf-girl awake?" Tristan asked as he came for a feel.

"Get away from me. Where is Vanessa?" I asked, glaring at him. The room was pitch black but I could still see him.

"Oh, honey, don't be like that. You sure got aroused by me before, and I know you will again. Vanessa is safe in another room," Tristan said as he caressed my body.

"You're a disgusting monster. I will never have sex with you again," I growled.

"Maybe not willingly," Tristan said, laughing as he slapped me across the face and proceeded to make his way out.

I was laying there in anger. I couldn't even imagine what they were doing to my sister. There was no way out this time. I could hear faint cries, and I knew she wasn't far. I couldn't protect her. Then I heard growls and screams. My door flew open and I couldn't believe it… was it Hunter?

Chapter 10

UNEXPLAINABLE

"Hunter, is that really you? Or am I just so weak that I'm hallucinating you?" I asked.

"No, I am here. I will explain everything, but we need to get you out of here," Hunter said as he ripped the restraints off me.

"What about Vanessa?" I asked.

"Damien has her," Hunter said as he picked me up. We ran out of the building and met up with the others outside in a brown van. Vanessa was out cold.

"Am I dreaming? I thought you guys died in that fire!" I asked as I looked around.

"Your mother and Rob decided they had no choice but to sacrifice themselves to save us. They did a very powerful spell, which left them behind," Hunter explained.

"No…" I said in tears.

"I'm sorry," Hunter said as he hugged me.

"I have had enough of them. They have ruined my life and now they are after Vanessa. They must be stopped," I snarled.

"We know. But Liz, you are weak and you need to feed," Hunter replied.

We stopped at a gas station on our way towards Ontario. We all got out of the vehicle to stretch, and that's when I noticed a human over by the door. I could hear his blood pumping through his veins, and I could smell his blood. I was sweating. I couldn't take it anymore. I ran towards him and shoved him against the wall. He was a young kid, maybe nineteen, wearing a black hoodie and blue jeans, and he wasn't very tall. I pinned him, biting into his neck. I couldn't stop myself. The kid screamed and kicked. As soon as I dropped the young boy to the ground, I was grabbed from behind and brought behind the gas station.

"What the hell! Hunter, what are you doing?" I asked as I pushed him.

"Liz, what am I doing? What are you doing? Are you insane? Killing someone in daylight like that? Do you really want to expose us? I guess that is what you do— changing into a werewolf and killing people, and now you're feeding on them where everyone can see." Hunter angrily glared at me.

"I'm sorry, I couldn't help myself," I snapped back.

"You need to do better at controlling it," Hunter replied.

"I know, next time…"

"There won't be a next time," Hunter growled as he rudely interrupted me.

I just stood there and looked at my angry brother. I had only seen him get mad a handful of times and they were all caused by my mistakes. I knew I needed to start being careful. The humans were already involved— we didn't need any more attention. How would I control my hunger, though? How did Hunter do it?

"How do you do it?" I asked.

"I hunt at night," Hunter replied. "Let's get moving. We don't have much time." He started walking towards the car. He stopped and walked back towards me.

"What's wrong?" I asked, shooting him a strange look.

"I have a bad feeling. I think they are close, so we need to get out of here. Damien will be meeting us in Ottawa," Hunter said as we bolted towards the car and sped off.

"Why is it so hard to kill those man-made hybrids? How are they so strong?" I asked, hoping Hunter would have some answers.

"I have no idea, but we need to figure out a way to get rid of them, as well as Caleb, once and for all," Hunter replied.

"I need to get drunk. Every time we defeat a monster, another stronger one just pops up. There is no use," I complained as I dozed off.

I woke up to Hunter shaking me. "Liz, wake up," he said.

"What?" I asked. I rubbed my eyes and looked out the window.

"We're here," Hunter said as he got out of the car.

"In a field? How is that safe?" I asked, puzzled.

"Just follow me," Hunter said.

I followed him down a path in the middle of an open field. There were no houses or any sign of civilization. We finally came to a huge tree. I looked at him funny. Hunter crawled into a huge hole, and I had no choice but to follow him. We ended up inside the tree trunk and I saw Damien, Vanessa, Celina, and Kelvin.

"Guys, it is so good to see you!" I shouted as I hugged everyone. I kissed Kelvin and picked up Celina. She was getting so big.

"Mama," Celina said as she giggled.

I started to tear up. "She called me mama."

Everyone chuckled at me.

"So what happens now?" I asked.

"Well, Vanessa will be shifting tonight. Her first transformation will be the toughest. She will be at her highest peak to tear things apart and her scent will be extremely strong. And knowing those other hybrids, they are not far behind and they will pick her scent up. So we need you and Hunter to cast a spell to smother her smell," Damien explained.

"Ok, that shouldn't be too hard," I said. I took a deep breath in and looked at Hunter.

It was only a few hours until the full moon, and we needed to act fast.

"Guys, why can't we kill those hybrids by using wolf's bane and silver?" I asked.

"That won't kill them. It will weaken them," Hunter replied.

"Yeah, and that will give us more time," I replied.

"Where do we get wolf's bane and silver? Then we are going to go purposely find them and try and stab them with a syringe? These hybrids are not stupid. We need a better plan. Right now we will just focus on Vanessa, then we will think of a plan to get rid of them," Hunter replied.

"You're right," I said as I glanced at Vanessa. "Her eyes just changed purple. It's starting," I said.

"Purple? Are your eyes purple?" Damien asked.

"No, mine are red," I replied. I looked at Damien.

"They were. Now they are purple," Damien replied.

"What does that mean?" I asked.

"It means you two girls are alphas," Hunter said.

"How is that possible?" I asked

"We will figure that out later," Hunter said.

We heard howls all around us; we were surrounded by wolves. Vanessa started screaming in pain.

"It hurts, make it stop!" Vanessa shouted as she held onto her stomach. Hunter and I started doing our spell to mask Vanessa's scent. As we started chanting it got really windy outside.

Vanessa was completely shifted—she was black. She sniffed her surroundings. "Guys, since Vanessa and I had a spell cast upon us that we wouldn't shift until we were twenty-four, what about Celine?" I asked as I looked at my baby. She stood up and waddled towards Vanessa. Vanessa growled, then tucked her tail in between her legs and started whining. She turned around and tried to escape. We did everything possible to have her trapped; we couldn't risk her being outside. She started howling, and her howls were a deep growl. The other wolves howled back.

"This is going to be a long night of babysitting," I muttered to myself.

"No one is asking you to be here," Hunter growled at me.

"Excuse me, but I am exhausted. I have been running from these monsters and I got tortured, so don't get pissy at me because I want a break!" I shouted back.

As Hunter and I were fighting, Vanessa managed to escape.

"Guys, Vanessa escaped!" Kelvin shouted.

"Great," I said as I got up and went outside. I couldn't even follow her scent due to that spell. I searched until daylight, but I had no luck. I decided I was going to jump tree to tree to see if I could find her from above. I spotted a body lying over in the open field. I jumped down and ran toward the body. It was Vanessa, lying there naked. I checked to see if she was ok. She had a faint pulse. I picked her up and put my jacket on her. She slowly woke up.

"What happened?" she asked.

"You shifted and you escaped. I have no idea what you did. I couldn't find you," I replied as we made our way back to our tree. Hunter was waiting for us. He helped me get Vanessa inside.

"We can't stay here. They will find us," Hunter said.

"Where do we go now?" I asked.

"Back to Edmonton. We will stay at my place," Hunter said.

"Ok, why?" I asked.

"Because they won't be expecting that. They will expect us to keep going east," Hunter explained as we all got up and walked towards our car. "Here, Damien, you take Vanessa, Liz and I will travel together," Hunter said as Damien guided Vanessa into his blue, two-door car.

"We will follow you, Hunter," Damien said.

We got into our designated cars and drove off.

Chapter 11

ECLIPSE

I was bored of sitting and not talking, so I tried to engage a conversation with my brother. "So I wonder what makes the full moon trigger a werewolf's transformation?" I asked.

"I don't know, but the eclipse is worse," Hunter replied.

I stared at him blankly. "Can you elaborate?" I asked.

"The eclipse is when the sun covers the moon for about an hour, and in that hour that makes us all very powerful and dangerous," Hunter explained.

"Ok, but when does that happen?" I asked.

"Tomorrow night. That is why we are trying to get everyone to a safe location so we can lock ourselves up, because if we get out, we are going to destroy anyone who gets in our path. Remember that whole conversation I had with you about exposing ourselves?" Hunter asked as he glanced over at me.

"Yes," I said.

"That would be a perfect night for us to get into trouble, and we can't have that," Hunter replied.

"I suppose that makes sense," I said as I turned on the radio.

I looked behind me, and I didn't see Damien but I saw a brown beaten-up truck behind us.

"Hunter— two problems. Damien isn't behind us, and there is an old truck speeding up behind us," I said. They hit our back end, making us jolt forward.

"Shit!" Hunter shouted as he sped up. The truck then pulled beside us and rammed into Hunter's door, causing him to swerve off into the ditch. He lost control and rolled the car a few times. I woke up and I was bleeding from my forehead. I looked over at Hunter he was unconscious. I kicked the door open with my knees, crawled out and made my way to the driver's side. I pried the door open and got Hunter out, shaking him and slapping him a few times. He slowly opened his eyes.

"What happened?" Hunter asked as he moaned in pain.

"A truck rammed into us, causing you to lose control and roll the car. I'm not sure who it was, but I don't think we have much time before they come after us again," I explained as I stood Hunter up. He could barely stand. "Are you ok?" I asked.

"Yes, I will heal. I need to phone Damien," Hunter replied.

"There will be no need for that," a man's voice shouted from the highway. It was Caleb. How did he always find us?

"You are all so easy to find," Caleb said, laughing.

Tristan and Mickey grabbed us and shoved us into the truck. We were both way too weak to fight back. "You guys are too easy to track. We caught Vanessa running wild last night in the fields. You guys did a poor job keeping a low profile on her, don't you think?" Caleb said as he chuckled.

"You can laugh all you want, but I will defeat you once in for all," I snapped back at him, shooting him a nasty glare through the ripped-up brown pleather seats. He looked back at me and smirked.

"You have tried numerous times to defeat me and you have never succeeded," Caleb said.

I just crossed my arms and looked out the window. I needed to figure out something. I didn't want to go back to their cold chambers and be tested on anymore. I was getting so tired of this shit. I looked over at Hunter. He didn't even move a muscle. It looked like he was in deep thought— either that or he was sleeping with his eyes open.

"So where are the others?" I asked, hoping they would tell me.

"If we told you that, it wouldn't be fun now, would it?" Caleb said as looked at me in the front mirror. "Tristan, turn here to the left up ahead," he demanded as he pointed to an old bumpy gravel road.

"Your truck probably can't even make it," I said, laughing. Just then we heard a wheel pop. Tristan swerved to the side, gently hitting a tree. The truck was smoking a bit, but no one got hurt. Everyone jumped out of the truck. I could smell wolf everywhere and they were pissed off. While Caleb and Tristan were checking it out I went over to Hunter. "Do you smell that?" I asked.

"Yes, they are very angry," Hunter replied.

"I know that, but who are they? What pissed them off?" I asked.

"Your guess is as good as mine. Look, we need to get out of here," Hunter said he took off running.

I didn't even second-guess him. I took off after him. I was mumbling to myself the whole way until I caught up to him. We ran as far as we could; we knew it wouldn't take them long to realize we were gone. We kept on the move.

"How the hell are we going to find the others and make it to Edmonton? We have no idea where we are, not to mention that we have two annoying hybrids on our ass all the time," I said as I looked around to see if I could figure anything out.

"I don't know all the answers. We will find a way. We always do," Hunter answered

We heard our names being yelled. They were not far behind, and we took off running again. I could hear growling all around us; it sounded like we were surrounded by werewolves.

"This can't be good," I said as I stopped in my tracks and smelled the air around me. They were hybrids. I could smell at least four. They stepped out of the forest and stood there growling at us. I growled right back, and my growl echoed throughout the forest. The hybrids backed off and let us through.

"You really are an alpha," Hunter pointed out as we headed towards the highway. We needed to hitchhike our way back. We sat on the side of the highway with our thumbs out. I was just about to give up when a white hummer pulled over to the side. The window rolled down and a gentleman with red curly hair and freckles covering his face greeted us.

"My name is Dennis, where you two heading?" Dennis asked, looking at us with his blue eyes. I noticed a young lady sitting in the passenger side. Her long brown hair covered her face and flowed down her blue top.

"We are heading towards Edmonton," Hunter replied.

"We are heading towards Saskatoon if you want a lift that far," Dennis said.

"Sure, that would be great," I replied as I opened the door and got in. Hunter followed behind me, and we sat down and did up our seat belts. It felt so good to be sitting down.

"Your names are?" Dennis asked.

"I am Liz and this Hunter," I answered.

"Nice to meet you two. This is my girlfriend Mandy. Sorry, she's sleeping," Dennis replied.

We made it to Saskatoon. My legs were cramping and I was hungry… I wanted to rip these two humans apart. They pulled up to a fairly nice brown-coloured apartment building.

"Well, you two, this is it. We hope you have a safe journey the rest of the way," Dennis said as he got out and opened the door for us. Hunter got out and I followed.

"Thanks a lot," I answered.

Hunter didn't even hesitate. He grabbed Dennis and pushed him up against the building, biting into his neck. Mandy started screaming.

"Shhh," I told her as I pushed her against the hummer and bit into her neck. We left their bodies and stole the hummer. We didn't have a lot time to get to Edmonton before Caleb caught up to us.

"So when we get into Edmonton, how are we going to get hold of Damien to see if he made it?" I asked.

"We will just go to our designated meeting area and go from there," Hunter replied.

I always loved it when we never really had a plan. It wasn't like our plans ever worked out, anyways. We made it just a little past Lloyd when a bunch of wolves went running across the highway, and one of them stopped in the middle of the highway causing Hunter to stomp on his brakes. These wolves looked terrified, like something was about to happen. I didn't have a very good feeling about this at all.

"What is happening?" I asked as I stared at the wolf. Its blue eyes stared at mine.

"I don't know, but it isn't good," Hunter responded as he undid his seat belt.

"Do you think it has anything to do with the eclipse?" I asked as I continued staring at the wolf.

"Possibly," Hunter said. He was just about to get out when the wolf just took off running. Hunter than quickly did his seat belt back up and we sped off again, only this time Hunter was really speeding.

"Slow it down! What is wrong?" I asked as I looked back.

"I don't like what is going on, and we need to get to Edmonton as soon as possible," Hunter replied. He started to slow down once we got further away from the incident.

We finally made it to Edmonton around midnight and went directly to our meeting grounds. We arrived at an old rundown building. The sides were covered in graffiti, and in front of the door stood a tall, well-built man. I couldn't help but notice a tattoo on his head, although I couldn't tell what it was.

"Hunter, really? This is our meeting place?" I asked as I looked at Hunter in disgust.

"Yes. We couldn't be picky, and we needed a place with protection," Hunter replied as he got out of the hummer.

I rolled my eyes and followed him. As we approached the man he put his hand out and commanded us to stop.

"We are here to meet with Gary. He is expecting us," Hunter replied.

The man spoke into his intercom and seconds later he moved out of our way and let us proceed through the doors. It smelled like cigarettes and marijuana. We went down a flight of stairs. It was dark and I was not liking this meeting place; everything about it was horrible. We stepped into a room filled with girls flocking over this guy who was sitting on a red leather seat. I couldn't really get a good look at him because there was a girl kissing him.

"Gary?" Hunter asked.

"Oh shit, you guys are here already. Girls, off," Gary commanded. The girls whined as they fled the scene. "Where is our little miss hybrid?" Gary asked as he stood up.

I stood there staring at him. He was tall like Hunter, and his blue eyes looked at mine. I thought his soul patch was so cute. He smiled at me, and his smile made me weak in the knees. He ran his hand through his black short hair. "You must be our Liz?" Gary asked.

"Yes, I am," I responded. I was really shy, but I didn't know why.

"You are beautiful. Now where is Damien?" Gary asked as he lit up a smoke.

"We don't know. We were hoping they were here already. We were thrown off track by Caleb. That's why we are late," Hunter replied.

"Ah, Caleb. How is that bastard doing? I hate that son of a bitch," Gary replied as he laughed a bit.

"He is as annoying as ever. He won't give up," Hunter replied.

"Well, and now that there are two female hybrids he will have twice the fun," Gary responded.

"Actually, there are three. Me, my sister Vanessa, and my daughter Celine," I explained.

Gary almost choked on his cigarette. "What, three?"

"Yes, trust me, I can count," I answered sarcastically.

"This isn't good," Gary answered as he paced back and forth

"What is wrong with three female hybrids?" I asked as I looked at Gary strangely. I knew I wasn't going to like the answer.

"I heard that if there was more than one female hybrid and if the government found out, shit was going to hit the fan especially because it is close to the eclipse. You and Vanessa are both their target. Celine is still too young, although your daughter is very powerful, Liz, more powerful than you yourself," Gary explained as he sat down on the couch and covered his face with his hands.

"Ok, so what happens to us?" I asked.

"I am not sure, but we need Vanessa and Celine here now," Gary answered.

"I don't even know where they are. Caleb wouldn't tell us. He gave me a sarcastic answer when I asked him where Damien and the others were," I replied. I could feel my anxiety rise.

I was getting lightheaded. The lights where bothering me, and I could barely stand anymore. I felt like I was going to faint. I had to hang onto the wall so I wouldn't fall down. I was sweating and breathing heavily. I could hear my heart beat faster and faster. I would try and open my eyes but I couldn't focus them.

"Liz, are you alright?" Hunter asked as he hung on to me.

"I don't feel so good. I think I have to sit," I replied as I sat over by Gary.

"I will go see if I can locate Damien. I have his scent. In the meantime, I want you to get some rest. Liz, the next few days are going to be something you will never want to experience again," Hunter said as he left the room

"This is going to be a huge war, and I am terrified," Gary said as he looked over at me. He could tell I was not well."You really look like you're dying. Can I get you anything?" he asked.

"I need to feed," I said as I slowly looked up at him. I could hear laughter coming from the other room.

"I know what you are thinking, and please don't," Gary said as he stood up. He tried blocking me.

"Get out of my way!" I snarled as I shoved him out of the way. He went flying and smashed into a wall, hitting his head on the cement flooring. He lay there unconscious. I looked at him and shrugged my shoulders. Just then a lady came from the other room to see what that noise was, and saw Gary laying there. I looked at her tall, slim body. Her brown wavy hair flowed down her back, and her bright red lipstick was all I could focus on. Her brown eyes were glaring at me.

"What did you do to him?" she asked as she walked towards him.

"He wouldn't move and I am hungry," I said as I ran up to her and knocked her on the floor. She started to scream as I bit into her neck. I couldn't stop myself. I stood up, wiping the blood off my mouth. There were at least four other girls standing there in shock. I was about to attack them when I was knocked to the floor.

"Get ahold of yourself— you're turning into a monster," Hunter said as he held me down.

"I just was having a little fun," I said, laughing.

"Hurting people is not fun," Hunter replied. "Leave, ladies, the show is over," he demanded. They left the room, and I could hear them talking about what just happened.

"You're no fun," I said as Hunter got up and helped me up too.

"What has gotten into you?" Hunter asked.

"Well, you said it yourself. I need to be prepared and that means being nasty, and I was hungry." I looked over at Gary. "What exactly is he?" I asked.

"Gary is a werewolf. You couldn't smell him?" Hunter asked, looking puzzled.

"No, I couldn't. Probably because I was not feeling well. I find when I am hungry my senses are low," I explained. "Did you find Damien?"

"Yes, they are almost here," Hunter replied.

I could feel anger rushing through me. I wanted to shift and rip everything apart. I felt so strong.

"Hunter, they better get here fast because if they don't I am going to shift and it's not going to be pretty," I said. I had to stop myself from turning.

"I know. I can feel the rush of anger go through me too," Hunter replied.

Soon Damien and the others came running through the door.

"What took you guys so long?" I asked.

"We had to take the long way. Caleb knew where we were," Damien replied.

"We need to get the wolves out of here and locked up," Hunter said as he picked Gary up and we headed downstairs to cellar. There were about ten chains hanging off the walls. It was freezing down there and it smelt like mold. Water was running down the walls onto the floor, and rats were running all over the place.

I was hanging onto Celine. She was getting so big. I was looking into her eyes and noticed them change purple like mine. "Her eyes just changed colour," I said.

"That is typical. She is probably going to change and it is going to hurt," Damien replied as he helped everyone get locked up. Vanessa and I were the only ones left to get chained up. We were about to get ready when we both started to turn… it was unstoppable. We shifted and crashed through a small window.

"Shit, no, this isn't good. I need to get out," Hunter shouted as he started to shift.

Damien stood there in fear; he didn't think the chains would hold them. He went running upstairs.

"Damien, how nice of you to run into us," Caleb said, laughing.

"Caleb. How come the eclipse isn't affecting you?" Damien asked.

"It has. I just can control it. Your little hybrids don't know how to control it. Speaking of hybrids, where are my girls?" Caleb asked as he looked into Damien's eyes.

"I don't know. They shifted and ran outside," Damien answered.

"Shit, we need to find them," Caleb snapped.

+ + +

Vanessa and I just ran, killing anyone in our way. We were out of control; we could hear screams and guns being fired, but we were too strong. We were not going down easily. I could smell blood everywhere, and it was making me more aggressive.

+ + +

"Are the others still locked up?" Caleb asked as he stepped outside and sniffed the air, trying to track us down.

"I think so," Damien replied, looking scared.

"You think so? Damien, that isn't a good enough answer. Go check!" Caleb commanded.

Damien went running back downstairs, only to find baby Celina still in her carriage. The chains were all snapped in half. Damien grabbed Celina and stormed back upstairs. "They're gone," he stated.

"You know what this means? It means all humans will now know we exist and they will stop at nothing to kill all of us. With four hybrids on the loose and out of control it is going to be a bloody massacre."

"How do you suggest we stop them?" Damien asked.

"We need to find them, but honestly I think it is too late," Caleb answered as he ran off.

Meanwhile, I could hear sirens and helicopters flying and circling us. Light was shining down on us, blinding me. I growled and ran out of the spotlight.

Two police officers were sitting behind their car trying to stay clear so none of us would see them. "What the hell are these things?" one of them asked.

"I don't know. I am going to sound like I am out of mind, but I think they are werewolves," the other police officer answered.

"How do we stop them?" one asked.

"You don't," Caleb said as he looked at them and smiled.

"Wwwho are you," the younger police officer asked as his brown eyes shook in fear. He pointed his gun at Caleb but his hands were trembling.

"That you don't need to know, and you can't kill me so how about you step out of the way and let me figure something out," Caleb replied as he shoved the officer aside.

I could feel myself getting weak as the night vanished and the morning was upon us. I growled at the others and we ran together to a nearby forest and shifted back. We lay there naked and cold; we were all too exhausted to move. I heard footsteps in the grass, and I tried to focus but everything was a blur. I woke up a few hours later and looked around. I was in a cell, and I was wearing some kind of scrubs. It almost looked like I was in jail.

Chapter 11

HELP

I stood there in shock, pacing back and forth. I didn't know what was happening or where the others were. I wanted to break free. I started yelling, hoping I would get someone's attention. I gave up and sat on my bed. I was a mess. I heard footsteps and I stood up and looked through the bars. It was an officer. He stood there smiling at me. His green eyes looked at me and he played with his brown goatee for a bit before he started harassing me. I was getting pissed off. I hate it when people interrogate me. He unlocked the cell and slowly stepped in, closing the cell door behind him.

"What do you want?" I snarled.

"Well, honey, you see, I want answers so I am going to ask you a few questions and pray that you don't lie to me. Ok, sweetheart?" the officer said as he came closer. His breath smelled like garlic and fish. I wanted to puke.

"Ok, but only if you step back or go brush your teeth," I said.

That pissed him off. "Look, bitch, what the hell are you?" the officer yelled.

"I am a girl," I answered.

He took his Taser out and shocked me. I fell to the ground in pain. I slowly got up and stared at him. He held his head and screamed in pain.

"You don't piss me off!" I yelled.

His screams brought attention to the other officers. They came running to his side, looked at me and shot me with a tranquilizer. I was out cold.

I woke up once again tied to a chair. The ropes were digging into my wrists, making me bleed. "Ok, I will cooperate. Just no more knocking me out," I replied.

"That's good. You came to your senses," a young man said as he stepped out of the shadow. I couldn't see his face, but his voice sounded raspy.

"So what are you? I know you're not human," the man asked.

"I think you already know what I am," I replied.

"I know, I know, but I want to hear it from you," the man demanded.

"I am a hybrid and a witch," I whispered.

"What was that, dear? You have to speak up," the man said as he stepped closer.

"Come closer," I said.

"You think I am stupid, little girl," the man replied as he backhanded me and left the room.

I struggled to get out, but the ropes where too tight and I was still weak. Moments after, the lights flickered on and three men stepped in. They threw Vanessa, Hunter, and Kelvin in. All three of them hit the cement floor.

"Now you will speak," the man with the raspy voice demanded. I could see who I was up against. He was tall, slim, scruffy and his brown hair was not well kept. The others were in bulletproof vests and their helmets covered their faces. They stood by the entrance holding guns.

"Are you going to answer or should I kill them?" the man hissed as he kicked Vanessa in the side. She yelped in pain.

"No, ok. I will tell you what you need to know. Just please don't hurt them," I begged.

"Good, now what are you?" he asked.

"We are hybrids and witches," I answered.

"What happened last night? You are responsible for killing a lot of innocent people," the man stated.

"The eclipse takes control of us and we do things we normally would never do," I answered.

"Unfortunately for you guys we have to put you down; we can't have you running around killing people," the man said. He nodded for one of the guys standing by the door to come over and help him. They injected Vanessa with a syringe, and her veins turned a red. She jolted a bit and closed her eyes.

"No!" I screamed as I struggled to break free, but the ropes dug in deeper.

Before they could inject anyone else there were loud screams coming from outside, and I could hear gunfire. Moments later the door flung open and there stood Damien and Gary. Damien was holding Celina. He put her down while he ran towards the guard standing by Vanessa. Damien slammed him against the wall and bit into his neck.

"You guys are too late. You will never get away alive," the man said as Mickey and Evan stepped in. They shifted into their wolf form. Gary shifted into a wolf form as well and they attacked each other.

"Now that they are occupied, shall we continue?" the man said as he laughed and walked towards me with a syringe.

"Get away from me, you sick fuck!" I snarled.

"Oh, sweetheart, I am not the sick fuck here!" the man hissed as he held me down with one hand so I would stop moving.

Just before he injected me Celine started to cry. Her crying did something to the enemies' hearing. The strange man and the two hybrids went down covering their ears.

"Someone shut that baby up!" the man snarled in pain.

Damien cut the ropes from my wrist and I was set free. I slowly made my way to Celina and picked her up. Gary shifted back and stole the guard's clothing. Damien and Gary went over to Hunter and Kelvin and helped them get up. We managed to escape and head back to Gary's place. Gary brought us a bag of blood so we could restore some of our energy.

"Vanessa... I have to go back for her," I said.

"You're not going anywhere," Damien demanded.

"You need to rest," Gary stated.

"What about Celina and her cry... what was that?" I asked. I looked over at her and she was sleeping.

"She is like you," Damien responded.

+ + +

Meanwhile, Mickey and Evan stood up. They looked over at the man, and he was still out.

"That baby's cry sure affected Chris," Mickey said, laughing.

"Great, now what are we supposed to do? We got one girl, but how are we going to get Liz?" Evan asked. He walked towards Chris and bent down and felt his pulse. "He is still alive, but I believe he will be out for a while," he said as he stood up and sighed.

"That's strange that Chris is still out; he is one of us," Mickey stated. He looked confused.

"You guys are not playing this smart at all. You are man-made hybrids—there is a big difference between man-made and the real deal," Caleb butted in. He stood in the doorway. He stared at Vanessa and shook his head. "What a shame. Why are you trying to kill these girls?" he asked.

"They are a threat to us, and besides, man-made hybrids will be the new deal. We will be the real thing soon." Mickey stated.

"Good luck with that. You have no idea how powerful Liz is, and don't forget her baby Celina," Caleb replied as he smirked a bit.

"You know something we don't?" Evan asked.

"Possibly, but I have already said too much," Caleb answered. He turned around and headed down the hallway.

"What, you can't just leave now?" Mickey shouted as he ran after Caleb. "How does he vanish like that?" Mickey asked as he looked around and growled. He made fists with his hands and punched a hole in the concrete wall. Blood ran down his hand and the wall cracked. "We will get those girls," Mickey snarled as he went back to where Vanessa and Chris were lying. Chris started groaning in pain, and he slowly stood up.

"What happened?" Chris asked.

"Well, you were about to inject Liz with that wolf's bane and her baby started crying and we all went down like a sack of potatoes. And as for you, I am not sure why it took you so long to wake up," Mickey replied.

"I am not sure. I need another injection, I feel weak," Chris demanded as he started to shake.

"We don't have anymore," Mickey said.

"You're lying, I need it!" Chris shouted as he slammed Mickey up against the wall and growled in his face. Mickey shoved, him causing Chris to go flying against the wall. Chris slowly got back up, rubbing his back. "What is happening to me?" Chris asked.

"Your body is rejecting the transformation," Evan spoke up. "I have never seen this, but I have heard about it."

"What does that mean? How do we fix it?" Chris asked.

"We can't," Evan answered.

+ + +

Meanwhile, I was dozing in and out. I had a hard time sleeping. I kept thinking about all those innocent people I had killed. I sat up and stared into space.

"Liz, are you alright?" Hunter asked.

"No, I am not. I killed a lot of people and I am not sure if I can cope with that," I replied. "I can't keep running from those man-made hybrids. Who was that man injecting us?"

"I'm not sure. I want answers too. I understand your pain, but you are strong. You can get through this," Hunter replied.

"I need help through this, and I don't know anyone that can help," I replied.

"You have us," Hunter pointed out.

Meanwhile, Chris just stood there feeling himself getting weaker.

"I need to get a boost somehow. What if I drink some of Liz's blood? Maybe we shouldn't kill her… what if her blood keeps us alive?" Chris seemed to be pondering some ideas. He didn't say anything else—he just walked out of the room.

"What is he doing?" Evan asked.

"I have a feeling he is going to find our little girl," Mickey replied.

"Chris, wait up! We need a plan. Or are you just going to go approach Liz in the state you're in and demand that she comes with you?" Mickey asked. Chris stopped in his tracks.

"I already have a plan. I am going to tell her that her little sister is alive and well… and it will be a trap," Chris answered. He smiled at Mickey and continued walking.

"That is actually not a bad idea," Evan stated.

+ + +

Meanwhile, I slowly got up and picked up Celina. I walked around the living room with her for a bit. I was terrified for her. I knew she was going to be even stronger that I was, and my life was in danger. I might have to give her up.

"Yeah, you're right, Hunter. Besides, I know that you guys have been there for me the whole time but I just feel like I am a burden," I said as I took a deep breath in. I kept looking at Celina.

"Don't think that way. We are family," Hunter replied as he went to hug me.

I ignored them and sat there in deep thought, just looking at my daughter. I didn't want this life for her.

"You guys, I am thinking I might have to give Celina up. I can't keep her safe. I can barely keep myself safe, and I just want the best for her," I announced.

"That is a huge decision. We will be there for you whatever decision you make," Hunter replied.

"I wouldn't even know who to give her to. I just don't know what to do," I said as I stared at Celina.

She just sat there dozing off and on; she was exhausted from all the running around we were doing.

"I can't just give her up to anyone. I need to trust whoever adopts my baby," I said as I felt anxiety take over my body. I was starting to get overwhelmed. I needed to step outside. "I am going out. Please do not follow me," I said as I got my purple sweater on, put my brown knee-high boots on and headed out the door.

+ + +

"I hate it when Liz leaves," Hunter said.

"Me too, but we can't control her. She will learn," Gary replied.

+ + +

I went and sat in a pub. I needed to unwind.

"What can I get you, miss?" the bartender asked me. I looked up at him. His bald head was covered in tribal tattoos, he had a bridge piercing and I noticed a wolf tattoo on his right forearm. His green eyes pierced through me.

"I will get the vodka special," I answered as I kept looking around. I was paranoid.

"Sure thing," he replied. Moments later he came back with it.

"Thanks," I replied as I gulped it back.

"Wow… you thirsty or just stressed?" the bartender asked as he chuckled a bit.

"You have no idea," I replied.

I got up and paid for my drink. I didn't really like being out in public, especially because the news kept playing footage of the night when I attacked all those humans. I think I was being paranoid, but people were looking me strangely like they knew it was me. By the time I left it was pouring rain. I wrapped my arms around my body and shivered a bit. I didn't get too cold, due to being a werewolf and all. I was just walking, minding my own business, when I heard screaming.

"Leave me alone!" I heard a young women's voice yell.

I ran over towards the crying and saw three young men wearing masks tormenting this poor girl. Her brown hair was dripping with water, and her white dressed was pressed up against her slim body. One man pushed her against an old broken-down fence and covered her mouth while the other two dug around in her purse.

"Hurry, Henry, find some cash and get the hell out of here before we are caught," the man holding the young women hissed. I went behind him and tapped him on the shoulder. He turned around and stared at me for a few seconds before saying anything.

"Shit, this bitch saw us!" he yelled.

"Don't worry, you won't get caught." I smirked as smiled at him. "Run!" I snapped at the women. She hesitated for a moment and ran away crying. "Now let's get down to business, shall we?" I said as I threw the man against the fence.

He flew through it, breaking the fence even more. I took a step forward when I heard a click towards my ear.

"I dare you to try and shoot me," I snarled, and stood there dead in my tracks.

"How the fuck are you so strong?" the guy asked as he held the gun. He was shaking so bad; I could smell the fear all over these men.

I was just about to turn around and steal the gun out of his hand when I heard another man's voice call out as he started to clap.

"Well, if it isn't Liz. What are you doing, saving the world? You know that isn't going to make up for what you have done," the man said as he crept closer.

"Caleb, don't you ever give up?" I asked, glaring at him.

The other three men took off running; they didn't want to stick around. I got their scent, so I wasn't too worried I would find them again.

"You just ruined my fun," I hissed as I walked past him.

"Not so fast, missy," Caleb growled. He grabbed my arm and held onto me.

"Let go of me!" I yelled, baring my teeth. "I am very pissy, so I suggest you don't fuck with me tonight." He held on tighter. I hated how he got a kick out of irritating me. He wasn't really a threat anymore; he was more annoying than anything, and always had bad timing.

"What got you so pissy?" Caleb asked as he smirked.

"None of your business," I snapped back. I tried to yank my arm away from him.

"Why can't you cooperate?" Caleb growled. He dug his nails into my arm, causing me to bleed.

"Because I don't need to listen to you. You are piece of shit!" I yelled. I used my mind to make him let go, and he slowly dropped to the ground holding his head. I turned around and just before I made a run for it, Caleb slid out a few more words. "I will get your baby. You don't know how valuable she is."

I took off running back home. I didn't stop. I was scared that something had already happened.

Meanwhile, back home, Hunter was holding Celina. "I wish Liz wouldn't take off. She always gets into trouble," Hunter said, staring at the clock.

"I know. We need to come up with a plan to keep Celina safe," Gary pointed out and they both heard the door fly open. I came crashing in and shut and locked the door behind me.

"Where the hell have you been?" Hunter asked, glaring at me.

"I don't have time to explain. We need to get Celina out of here. Caleb is after her. Gary, you take her far away and don't let anyone know where you are going. Here, have my grandmother's crystal necklace she gave me. It's good luck. I will cast a spell on it to protect you both, but you need to leave. She isn't safe here." I was shaking so bad. I was scared, and I knew something bad was going to happen.

"Liz, are you sure?" Gary asked. He hugged me.

"What choice do I have? I can't keep her safe," I whispered.

I didn't know what was going to happen or how I was going to keep myself safe— all I knew was I needed to get Celina far away. I was in for a surprise and I hated surprises.

Chapter 12

ENDING THIS NIGHTMARE

"I will pack up and leave first thing tomorrow morning," Gary said.

"No, you need to leave now. Look, I ran into Caleb and before I made my escape he told me he will get Celina, so there is no waiting. "We don't have time," I said as I ran my hands through my wet hair. I paced back and forth, just repeating "we don't have time."

"Ok, I will take her tonight," Gary said as he packed up stuff for the both of them.

I was so mad I started throwing things around the living room, causing Celina to cry.

"Calm down!" Hunter shouted as he pushed me against the wall and growled in my face. I stopped and broke down crying. Hunter just held me.

"We are ready to leave," Gary said

I sniffled and wiped my eyes. "Take care of her, please, and don't let anyone know anything. Celina, I love you and I am sorry I have to do this. You will understand one day, but this is for the best. You be good for Gary," I said as I kissed her forehead. She started smiling. "Goodbye, Celina," I whispered as I watched Gary take my baby out the door.

Not even half an hour after they left, Caleb and Mickey came crashing through my door. I was so mentally drained I just sat on the couch glaring at them. "You guys are too late," I said, grinning.

"No, you bitch!" Mickey snapped, slapping me across the face.

"Leave her alone," Hunter growled.

"Or what?" Mickey asked as he laughed.

"What do you really want? I mean, is this all about your man-made hybrids? Frankly, I am getting sick of his running away shit," I demanded.

"Yes, but we want your baby. She is more powerful than you are. As for you, we just like to torment a hot-looking hybrid," Mickey growled.

"You are fake, and you will never get my baby!" I yelled. I stood up. "Get out," I demanded as I stared into his eyes. His eyes started bleeding.

"What the hell," Mickey snarled. He looked at his bloody hands, looked at me and ran out the door.

Caleb stopped and stared at me for a few minutes before speaking. He smirked and put his hand on my face. I grabbed his wrist and twisted it. He ripped his arm away from me, and before he left he said, "This would have been way easier if you just would stop fighting."

I didn't say a word. I glared at him while I watched him leave. He slammed the door shut, causing the door frame to crack.

"Fuck! I can't take it anymore! We need to kill them and make sure they are dead. They will find Celina, I know it!" I shouted as I picked up my table and threw it across the kitchen floor. It smashed against the wall, breaking in half while leaving a huge hole in the wall. I fell to the floor crying.

"Do you feel better?" Hunter asked as he knelt down beside me, patting my back.

"No, I am super frustrated and I am going to come up with a plan to destroy Caleb and those wanna-be hybrids," I hissed. I stood up and stared at the wall I had damaged earlier, deep in thought.

"Are you ok?" Hunter asked as he patted my shoulder.

"Yeah, just thinking of a way to defeat them. We need to catch them off guard. I don't know how, but I need to come up with a spell to bring their defenses down," I explained as I took the cushion off my couch. I had left one of my spell books there earlier. I put the book down on the floor and started searching for a certain spell. I came across a spell called "defeat those who shall never succeed." That one is perfect," I said as I flipped to page 101.

"I am sorry to burst your bubble, sis, but we are the only hybrids left against Caleb and three other hybrids. How do you think this is going to work?" Hunter pointed out.

"Do you have a better idea?" I hissed as I continued to read the spell. It said: *On a full moon you will need the blood of a witch and a werewolf. Place the blood in a pot with wolf's bane and silver. Wait until midnight and start chanting.*

Defeat those who shall never succeed

Keep away unwanted ones

As you are nightmares on my soul

You shall be gone for ever and never to come back

Your shadows desist
Defeat those who shall never succeed

It also stated that the enemies would remain as stone forever. I closed the book and stood up. "Easy enough for me," I said with a smile.

"When exactly did you want to do this?" Hunter asked nervously.

"Next full moon, which is tomorrow night," I said.

"I have a bad feeling, but I guess I am with you," Hunter replied.

I was tired, but I knew I wouldn't be able to sleep not knowing. I had a huge plan and it wasn't going to be easy, but I had to get it done. I wanted to be safe for once. I was exhausted from running, and I wanted my baby safe. I had lost too much and enough was enough.

Meanwhile, Mickey was washing the blood from his face, and he was swearing as he was doing so. "Why is she so stubborn? She is always one step ahead of us," he muttered as he inspected his face for more blood.

"She is quiet, the girl, I must say... very brave," Caleb replied.

"We need to get her baby, and then we can use her baby against her," Mickey said as he started grinning. "We need to track her. She couldn't have made it far."

"I can do a tracking spell," Caleb pointed out.

"Great. Let's get on it. The longer we wait, the harder it will be to find them," Mickey stated. They left the bathroom of the old, rundown gas station. It was hot and windy out, with dust blowing everywhere.

"Where are we going?" Caleb asked. He looked up and the sun almost blinded him.

"Somewhere out of the sun, for starters," Mickey replied as he headed towards a big willow tree with its long draping leaves touching the ground. "This should do it," he stated as he sat under the tree.

Meanwhile, I kept tossing and turning in my sleep, and I woke up covered in sweat. I sat up panting, wiping my forehead. Hunter woke up and gave me a concerned look.

"I had a nightmare that they found Celina and I was too late; it seemed so real," I said as I held onto my stomach. I couldn't breathe... the thought of them finding her frightened me.

The wind outside blew the branches, causing them to scrape across my windows. I could hear dogs barking just a few houses down, and I just sat there in silence. Everything around me stopped as I couldn't catch my breath.

"I am sure she is safe. It was just a nightmare," Hunter reassured me as he lay back down.

"No, you don't understand. It was real, it was a warning," I said as I stood up and got my jacket on.

"Where are you going now?" Hunter got up.

"I am leaving. I need to find those two monsters and stop them before they find her," I explained as I got my boots on.

"You are so stubborn, but I am not letting you do this alone," Hunter replied as he got his jacket and shoes on. We headed out the door, which the wind nearly ripped off its hinges.

"It's so windy out here," I complained. I walked with my head down.

"No doubt," Hunter agreed.

Tomorrow was the full moon, and I had no idea what I was doing or what I was in for, but I would try anything to stop those monsters from winning. Enough was enough, and I wanted them gone for good. They already killed my sister and she didn't even stand a chance. Every day that passed I grew stronger… I could feel it. I caught myself thinking about Gary and Celine… like, where are they? I hoped they were safe. What if they found them? Gary wasn't strong enough to stand up to them; he was just a werewolf. I had to find them. I knew something was wrong, I could feel it.

I kept to myself as Hunter and I walked down the middle of the road with the rain pouring down. It was so quiet for a city— hardly any vehicles, no dogs barking, no birds chirping. All you could hear was the rain coming down and hitting the rooftop of buildings and vehicles. I knew Hunter did not agree with this plan, but as always he had to make sure he followed me.

"You know, even if you defeat these monsters you will never be safe. There will always be an enemy. That is just the way it is," Hunter said, his voice getting sterner.

"I know, but at least Celina would be safer for a little bit longer," I replied.

"You can't always protect her," Hunter said.

"I don't want to talk about this anymore. I brought her into this world. I need to make sure she is fine. I am not allowing those freaks to get their grubby hands on my daughter," I snapped.

"I completely understand where you are coming from, but she is safe. You need to trust Gary," Hunter replied as we kept walking aimlessly. "Do you know we are going?" Hunter piped up before I could get a word in.

I didn't say anything for a few moments because I had no idea where I was going. I was just hoping I would find a scent.

"Well," Hunter spoke up again, except this time he sounded aggravated.

"No, I have no idea where I am going," I whispered in embarrassment.

Meanwhile, Gary was lost and had no idea where he was taking Celina. They stayed in a hotel just outside Rapid City. It was dirty, and the vacant sign was burnt out. It looked like a hotel from a horror movie. Gary shuddered every time he had to enter the room. Celina was sitting in front of the TV watching cartoons when she heard something. She slowly got up and made her way to the window. She stared out and started to cry.

"What is it, Celina?" Gary asked as he approached the window. It was drizzling a bit, but not too hard. The sun was trying to peek through some of the gloomy clouds. Gary saw a figure run across the parking lot. He then saw the door knob jiggle. Celina stared at the door. The door knob kept jiggling but whomever was trying to break in couldn't.

"What the hell!" the deep voice yelled out.

"We know you're in there, Gary. I will come through that window if I have to!" the man yelled.

"How did Mickey and Caleb find us so fast?" Gary asked himself. "I am not strong like they are… I am only a werewolf."

Mickey walked towards the window and tried smashing the glass with his fist. Nothing. His fist just bounced off. "What the…" Mickey said to himself as he looked through the window at Celina.

"What is happening, break the glass!" Caleb yelled as he tried using a spell to break the glass. It was that stupid baby, he thought.

Gary looked down at Celina. She wasn't doing anything unusual; she was just standing there sucking her thumb and giggling occasionally.

The wind started to pick up, blowing dust around the parking lot and making it hard to see those two monsters outside. I close my eyes and opened them. When I opened them I noticed we were right in front of Liz and Hunter.

"Gary, Celina. How is this possible?" I asked, surprised. I looked at both of them and rubbed my eyes to see if I was sleeping, but nope, they were still standing there in shock.

"I think your child is very powerful," Gary said. He told us what happened back at the hotel in the States.

"That is why they are after her," I said as I hugged myself. It was getting very cold out, and I couldn't stop chattering. "I guess we can go back to my place," I said.

"Probably not a great idea. As soon as they find out we are not in the hotel anymore they will transport right back here," Gary pointed out.

"Well, where do you suppose we go?" I asked. I shrugged my shoulders in frustration.

"Anywhere but here," Gary said, not helping the situation at all.

"That was helpful… any takers?" I asked as I looked at Hunter.

"Don't look at me, sis," Hunter replied as he shot me a confused look.

"So we're just going to stand here in this freezing weather? At least we can be a warm place if they are going to find us," I snarled as I wrapped my arms around my body in at attempt to keep warm.

"I don't know what to tell you. We are all just as lost as you are," Hunter replied.

The air was crisp and the wind was loud. The whistling sound hurt my ears. My hair blew around, whipping me in the face. I was worried about my baby freezing, but every time I looked at her she didn't seem to be bothered by the weather.

"I hate to break it to you, but you do realize they will find us no matter where we run. I think it's time we stand up to the battlefield and fight," Gary said. He stopped in his tracks and looked at me, waiting for me to say something. I just stared back.

"I know, but I am not ready. I have no idea what we are up against. This could be huge. I would need to practice my magic, and what if I am not strong enough?" I asked as I started to tremble in fear.

"Liz, look at me! You are the most powerful hybrid. You have to believe in yourself," Gary snarled at me. "You have made it this far, you have family and friends who are willing to stand by your side.""I know you are right, but I still need to come up with a game plan," I said.

Celine started to do something strange… there was a glowing light around her. It was so bright I couldn't see. I just dropped to the gravel road and covered my eyes. It lasted about a minute. I slowly looked back up and my baby wasn't there. Instead, there was a young, beautiful woman standing there. Her brown wavy hair fell off her shoulders, and her brown eyes wandered restlessly. She looked down at her hands and then looked at me.

"Mom, what is going on?" Celina asked as she looked at Hunter and Gary.

"You're growing up," I answered, just as confused as her. I had no idea how. I was guessing it was because of her powers.

Chapter 13

CELINA

I just stood there in shock. I couldn't believe it. My Celina was able to talk and walk on her own. Never mind that, she was a young woman. She had no idea what was going on. I had to teach her and help her understand how powerful she really was.

"My god, she is beautiful," Gary said as he looked at Hunter and I and back at Celine.

"What now?" Celine asked, shrugging her shoulders.

"I need to explain what you are and what you are capable of, sweetie," I answered as I smiled.

"Maybe we should get out of here before they catch up to us," Hunter interrupted.

"That is too late. We were drawn to Celina's powers," Caleb replied, laughing as he lunged for Celina.

Celina raised her hand and Caleb went flying. She stared at him as he skidded on the dirt road. "I have had enough of your nonsense. This ends now!" Celina shouted as she raised both her arms. It started to get very windy, and I looked over at Caleb and Mickey, who were screaming in pain. Blood poured down their eyes and ears. They begged her to stop. She couldn't control her powers, and she proceeded to torture them as they lay in their pools of blood screaming.

I couldn't say anything. I just watched her torture them. I was fascinated by their pain. They caused me so much pain by killing my family. I was so angry. I stood closer to her and joined her, sure this would be enough to kill them. Finally not having to deal with these monsters anymore got me so excited. The screams became more intense, and then they stopped. Celina and I stopped and walked towards the lifeless bodies of these monsters. They were not moving and they were surrounded by blood. I felt ecstatic.

"Did we kill them?" Celina asked as her whole body started to shake.

"I...I don't know," I responded as I went closer to the bodies. I bent down to feel for pulses, but nothing. "It appears that we did," I replied as I looked over at Celina.

"Mom, I am so sorry. I don't know what happened," Celina apologized, sighing.

"I will tell you what happened. You were out of control. You are dangerous," Hunter snapped as he looked at me.

"How dare you say that—she has no idea what is happening to her. It took me a long time to control my urges. Look at the life I have lived. And you think you have the right to judge her!" I shouted. I got back up, went towards my brother and slapped him across the face. I walked away in anger.

"Liz, wait," Gary said. He was about to take a step forward when Hunter grabbed his arm. "Let her be," Hunter replied.

"Mom, wait, "Celina shouted as she ran after me.

"Let the girls be," Hunter said as he looked over at Caleb and Mickey.

"Mom, what is going to happen now?" Celina asked as she brushed her hair behind her ear.

"I don't know. I never know," I said. I looked over at her and smiled.

"Were you scared?" Celina asked.

"Very. I still am. I don't know what else is out there just waiting to torture me. I live day by day— that is all I really can do," I replied.

+ + +

"Well now what, Hunter?" Gary asked as he shot Hunter a pissed-off look.

"Don't look at me that way. It's not my fault Liz and Celina took off," Hunter replied.

"You started it. You ran Celina down and got Liz pissed off. You know pissing the original hybrid off isn't the smartest thing to do," Gary snapped. He was about to turn around and start walking but something grabbed him and threw him against a tree. He dropped to the ground and slowly got up.

"Well, if isn't the hybrid and his pet wolf. Where is your sister?" the strange man asked. He was wearing a black jacket. His black hair blew in the wind and his red eyes pierced the night.

"Who the hell are you?" Hunter growled as he bared his fangs.

"I am sorry. How rude. My name is Gavin and I am a… let's say a very old hybrid who has been looking for Liz for a very long time," Gavin replied. He smiled, showing off his white fangs.

"I would never tell you," Hunter hissed.

"Very well then," Gavin replied in a soft, calm tone as he shifted into a werewolf. Hunter's jaw dropped. He had never seen a werewolf like this before. He was a black wolf, at least nine feet tall with red beady eyes, huge fangs, and a scar on his nose. He growled at Hunter and crouched down in front of him.

+ + +

Celina and I were walking when I dropped to the ground.

"What is it, Mom?" Celina asked.

"It's Hunter. He is in trouble," I replied as I shot around and ran towards him. I could always tell when he was in trouble. "Hold up," Celina said as she followed closely behind me.

When I reached Hunter and Gary, I stopped in my tracks. I shocked to see such a huge werewolf.

"Enough!" I shouted at the wolf.

It stopped and stared at me. It felt like I was glued to that spot. The wolf started shifting back into a human and became a man with black hair and brown eyes. He stared at me and smiled, walking towards me.

"Don't fucking come near me until you explain who you are and what you want!" I growled as I backed up against a tree.

"Oh, honey, you don't have to be afraid. My name is Gavin and I am a very old hybrid," Gavin proceeded to explain to me. "I have been waiting a very long time to meet up with the first female hybrid." He stared into my blue eyes.

He scared me. There was something about him that was so dark. I didn't trust him.

"What do you want with me?" I asked as I tried to move but he had me pinned up against the tree

"I want you, my dear," Gavin said as he touched my cheek. His hand was cold.

"I will pass," I said as I pushed him out of the way.

"It doesn't work that way. If I were you I would do this the easy way because you don't want to piss me off. Now be a good little girl and come with me," Gavin hissed as he grabbed my arm.

"Don't touch me, you disgusting excuse for a werewolf!" I yelled. I raised my hand and sent him flying onto the dirt road.

It was so cold out, the rain was pouring, the wind was screaming in my ears and I had a pounding headache.

"Oh my, you are good, but I know that you are a witch and you can't kill me like you did Caleb and Mickey," Gavin said as he stood back up.

"How did you know they are dead?" I asked.

"I was Caleb's partner for the longest time. Him and I worked together to make these hybrids using humans to hold the DNA of werewolf and vampires, but it only worked for a selected few— the rest died due to the rejection. Caleb told me he found you, but you were always too strong and sneaky. So after I learned he was dead, I took the opportunity to find you myself without anyone getting in the way," Gavin explained. He looked over at Celina. "Ah, yes, this is your daughter. My, my, she is gorgeous… just like her mother."

"Mom, I'm scared," Celine said as she came over to me.

"If you come with me, lady, I will leave your family alone. If you choose not to I will destroy your whole life," Gavin said.

"Fine!" I yelled as I looked at Celina.

"No, Mom, you can't," Celina replied as she started to cry. "I can't do this alone."

"Yes, you can. You are so strong. You just need to believe in yourself," I said. I kissed her cheek.

"Are you out of your mind?" Hunter and Gary both asked at the same time. "Do you have any idea what is going to happen?" Hunter asked.

"Yes, but it will keep you guys safe," I replied.

Celine started screaming and crying on the top of her lungs. "I will not have you take my mother," Celine snarled, and she started to shift.

"You are a silly girl," Gavin said, laughing as he shifted

I looked at Hunter and Gary and smiled. We all shifted. Growling at Gavin, we took off after him. Gavin swung at Hunter, causing Hunter to slam right into a tree whimpering. He got back up shaking, growling and attacking once again. I leaped on Gavin's back, biting his neck, and he growled and knocked me off. I hit the ground and slid. Celina pinned Gavin to the ground, leaving him paralyzed. Gavin shifted back into human, smiled and sped off into the forest. We all shifted back, looking at each other and wondering what the hell just happened.

"Besides being naked, how is everyone holding up?" I asked as I tried to cover up.

"How are we going to get clothing?" Celina asked.

"We can speed off into town and grab clothing. No one will even see us," Hunter suggested.

"What about me? I am not a vampire, I am just a werewolf," Gary replied.

"Oh yeah, well, stay here and we can grab you clothing too," I said.

"That's a great idea. Stay here with that Gavin dude," Gary snarled.

"Well, I am sorry, but I think that is the best idea right now, unless you have better one," I said.

"I guess you're right," Gary said as he crossed his arms.

"We will be right back," I said.

We took off into town and tried to be as fast as we could. We broke into a nearby store. We set off the alarm, but we were in and out.

+ + +

Gary was just standing there minding his own business when he heard something in the forest behind him. He swung around, his eyes glowing red, but he saw nothing. Slowly turning back around, he saw Gavin standing there smiling.

"Now, Gary, you are going to cooperate with me or I will kill you," Gavin said as he ran his nail down Gary's cheek.

"Ok, I will listen, I promise… just don't kill me," Gary said as he started to sweat.

"Good choice." Gavin smirked. He wrote a note, pinned it to a tree, and took off with Gary.

+ + +

We got back and stopped… we could smell that something wasn't right.

"Where is Gary?" I asked. I yelled his name and nothing.

"Look over there on that tree. There's a note," Hunter said, pointing.

We walked towards it and it read: "If you ever want to see your precious Gary again meet me at the Red River park at midnight. Love Gavin."

"I should have ripped his throat open when I had the chance," I said as I tore the note up.

"How are we going to get Gary back safely?" Celina asked.

"I don't know just yet," I replied.

"Well, we need to think of something fast. Who knows what that freak will do with him," Hunter stated.

"We are idiots… we can use magic! All three of us are witches," I explained. "We can use a cloaking spell to get Gary out, and in the meantime I can deal with Gavin." I smiled.

It was about 5 am and the sun was just coming out. None of us had slept or eaten anything. What was I getting myself into? I was so exhausted… when would this end?

Chapter 14

THE BATTLE

Here we were walking to save yet another friend. My life was always revolving around saving someone. We managed to sniff out Gary's scent and follow his scent right to a gas station.

"This is strange," I said, puzzled.

"Well, let's go inside," Celina said as she strutted for the front door.

We all followed behind her. I had a bad feeling about this, but if this was where Gary was then we had no choice but to go inside. We opened the door, trying to be quiet, but the door let off this horrible screeching noise. You could tell this place hadn't been used for a while. There were cobwebs everywhere, and the dust was so thick you could hardly see the shelves. The smell was nasty… it smelled like gas and fish. Coming across an old freezer, I opened it up and found to my surprise that there was indeed still fish in there. I started to gag. I shut the freezer door and walked towards the back.

"This place is gross," Hunter whispered as he tried to cover his nose.

"The sooner we find Gary, the better," I replied.

We heard noises coming from downstairs. We froze to see if we could hear what or who it was.

+ + +

"Well, Gary, I wonder if your little Liz is going to come save you?" Gavin said as he crouched down beside Gary.

"Yeah, she will be here, and you will not get away with this," Gary snarled.

Gavin laughed and decked Gary in the face, causing him to fall over, still strapped in a wooden chair.

+ + +

"I think they are downstairs," I said as I flew down the stairs, leaving Celina and Hunter behind.

"I hate it when she does that," Hunter said to Celina as they bolted after me.

I entered a dark room. It was all dirt with no lights, and it was cold. I turned on my wolf eyes to have a look around and saw Gary down on the ground trying to rock side to side.

"Gary," I said as I ran towards him. I helped him out, ripping the ropes off him.

"Gavin did this," Gary said.

"I know, I found a note where he took you," I said.

"Liz, can you please not run off like that anymore?" Hunter said as he shot me a dirty look.

"I am sorry, I just needed to save Gary," I explained as I helped Gary up.

"Going so soon?" Gavin asked as he walked into the room, bumping right into me.

"Get out of my way," I growled. I shoved him aside, holding Gary up at the same time.

"Don't be like that. Besides, I have been waiting a very long time for this, and I am not losing you again," Gavin said with a stern voice. He grabbed Gary out of my arms and threw him, causing him to skid across the dirt ground.

"No, Gary!" I yelled as I tried to run towards him, but Gavin had too strong of a grip.

"We got him," Hunter said as he ran towards Gary.

"Take him and leave. I will be right behind you," I replied, looking at Gavin.

"We will see about that," Gavin said as he got even angrier.

The others took off with Gary. They knew they had to trust me on this one. If they stayed, they would have made matters worse and I didn't want anyone else to get hurt. I didn't have any plans, but I knew what I had to do.

"You sound pretty sure that you are going to escape this. You see, darling, you have two choices— either you come with me or you don't leave at all. Your call," Gavin stated as he touched my face.

I backed away in disgust. "I am not going with you. As far as I know, you are a monster," I snarled. I waved my hand up, causing him to slam into the wall.

He growled and slowly got back up, wiping the dirt off him. "You are not going to make this easy on me are you?" Gavin asked as he leaped towards me.

I moved out of the way and slammed into the wall. I held his hands behind his back and pushed his head into the wall. "You are going to listen to me. I am going to make myself very clear. I do not want anything to do with you ever, so leave me, my family, and my friends alone," I snapped. I moved away from him.

"You know, I was going to make this easy on you, but since you seem to like it rough, I can play that too," Gavin replied, laughing. He turned around and grabbed me by the throat, lifting me in the air. I started kicking my legs. I couldn't breathe. I swung back and forth a bit and was able to kick him the face, causing him to drop me. He yelled and fell to the ground holding his face.

"You bitch," Gavin snarled as he started to shift.

"I am not in the mood for this," I replied. I lifted my hand and sent Gavin flying into the wall. Blood ran down his face, and he was unconscious. I went over to him and kicked him. Nothing. I shrugged and ran out of the building. I met up with everyone outside and I stared at the old building until it set on fire. "Let's see Gavin escape this," I said, laughing. When I turned around, I ran right into Gavin. He was staring at me with his blood-red eyes gleaming. He looked like he was going to tear my face off at any moment. His skin was covered in black ash, and he stunk like burning flesh. I was sure I had ended this nightmare. How did this happen? How did he escape?

"You look surprised, sweetheart. Did you actually think a little fire could stop me?" Gavin asked. He grabbed my neck and held me up high, my feet dangling and kicking. I couldn't breathe. I held up my hand to hit him with that screeching noise, but nothing.

"What's wrong? Your magic isn't working?" Gavin asked as he threw me across the dirt ground.

I got up coughing and holding my neck. I gasped for air as I slowly regained my stance. "How did you escape?" I asked. I dreaded the answer.

"You underestimate me. I am much stronger than you think," Gavin smiled, showing off his white teeth. "I must say, you are a brave young girl." He walked toward me.

"I don't understand… how did you take my magic?" I asked as I backed up.

"If I told you, that wouldn't be fun now, would it?" Gavin asked. He grabbed me and threw me the ground, holding my head down.

"Leave her alone!" Hunter snarled as he ran toward Gavin. As soon as Hunter went anywhere near Gavin he went flying backwards.

"Leave my mother alone!" Celina shouted, and she started screaming.

"Don't cry, my dear, your turn will be next. Oh, how I love female hybrids," Gavin said.

Celina yelled so loud the ground started to shake. Gavin fell off me in pain. I turned around and kicked him in the face, and I could hear his neck snap. He fell to the ground, blood dripping from his nose.

"Well, I don't think the bastard is dead, so we better get moving," I said as I grabbed Celina's arm and trotted past the guys.

I stopped in my tracks and stood there for a second.

"What are you doing?" Celina asked, looking at me funny.

"I am the strongest hybrid. I am tired of running. I am going to end this once and for all," I replied as I headed back towards Gavin's lifeless body. I started chanting some words over and over again. His body shot up in flames. I watched him burn until his body was ashes.

"I think he's dead," Hunter said.

"Let's hope so. I am exhausted. Let's go home," I said. I held Celina's hand.

"Do you know what happened to the red diamond?" Hunter asked.

"I thought Mom put a spell on it so no one could touch it. Honestly, I think the boys forgot about it… they were too busy chasing me," I said, laughing.

"We should make sure," Hunter replied.

"How? Our house is burned down, and besides, I don't want to waste my breath worrying about anything anymore," I explained as I let out a big sigh.

"I suppose you're right," Hunter agreed.

We had no idea where we were going, but I was sure my adventures were not over with yet. My life had changed so drastically, but I had survived everything. I was a little worried to see what else awaited me. I had lost so much, but I had gained so much.

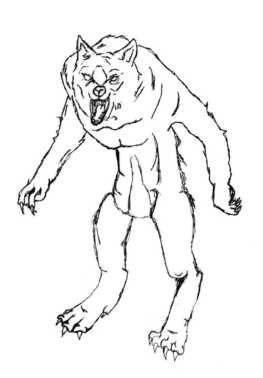

CPSIA information can be obtained
at www.ICGtesting.com
Printed in the USA
LVOW12*0043030218
564915LV00006BB/66/P